Fiona Cooper is the author of *Rotary Spokes*, *Not the Swiss Family Robinson*, *Heartbreak on the High Sierra*, *The Empress of the Seven Oceans* and *Jay Loves Lucy* (which is also published by Serpent's Tail). She lives in Newcastle on Tyne.

I Believe in Angels

Fiona Cooper

'Fugue' first appeared in *Writing Women*, Christmas 1990. 'Brightly Shone the Moon That Night' first appeared in *The Plot Against Mary* (The Women's Press, 1992).

Library of Congress Catalog Card Number:

A catalogue record of this book is available from the British Library on request.

First published 1993 by
Serpent's Tail, 4 Blackstock Mews, London N4
and 401 West Broadway #1, New York, NY 10012

Typeset in 10½ Galliard by
Contour Typesetters, Southall, London

Printed in Finland by Werner Söderström Oy

Contents

For Jean, who walks and talks with angels

Aubade: The Maggots of Enlightenment

· ·

'**M**aggots! Look at them! I've seen maggots brown, I've seen them white, I've seen them red and *crawling*, but I never seen *nothing* like this in my life before! Look!'

And it was only seven-thirty. In the morning. The time when you would be relieved by the spectre of a hansom cab in the eerily unpeopled streets. There was only chill grey mist, and sooty buildings vanishing some two floors up. If there's sky on a winter morning in England, I've yet to see it. There's something in them thar clouds. I have this theory it's frozen mist all the way to outer space. But no matter, and who am I to complain, certainly not to Jan, the lady of the maggots, who has been up since four and already whisked through acres of office carpet, scads of bins and oceans of scummy cups.

I had this job, you see, looking after children at the Zephandra Butolphi Community of Enlightenment. Zephandra Butolphi I'd never seen and neither had most of the *butis* — Jan says booties — who lived there. But they lived in hope that they might be so blessed. He operates from Southern California and sends words of hope and encouragement worldwide. There was a shelf full of his books in the Communing Room where they eat, meditate, and experience ecstasy. I picked up a couple once — *The Dawning of Extraordinary Being* and *The*

Zigzag Path of Super-Zen. Couldn't make out a damn thing from either one of them. Zephandra Butolphi has this idea that you have to repeat everything until it becomes *one with the cosmic miasmal consciousness*, so pages one, two and three read: '*the dawning, the coming of light, the evanescence of new being, the dawning, the coming of light, the evanescence of* . . .' Etcetera etcetera.

But I didn't mind the butis, they seemed pretty harmless. And they employed me.

There were twenty-seven butis in the Community, and they lived in this ought-to-be-condemned building off Stoke Newington High Street. They had a thing for brown: brown robes, brown carpets, brown rice. My mother said brown doesn't show the dirt but she never saw this house. They looked after about fifteen children from dawn to dusk and it was in their belief to take in and embrace all children in the love and light of Zephandra Butolphi. So we would get a screaming phone call from one of the local nurseries, and ten minutes later a howling, sopping bundle lands on the doorstep and the welcoming buti scoops it up, sick and nappies and all. The other crèches thought we were nuts, but useful, and since they relied on government funds, and the butis worked on spontaneous gifts of love and the sale of silk flowers, we had outlasted most of them. We got along really fine. Some of the children had done every nursery in N16 and couldn't believe that they wouldn't be shifted again.

Well, with twenty-seven enlightened butis and fifteen children, you might ask what they needed with an under-the-counter unqualified Yankee nursery assistant like me.

Zephandra Butolphi must have been a civil servant in a previous incarnation: no one ever made a decision alone. Which meant that the butis had total Community meetings to come to a 'synthesized accord' whenever the need was felt. And some buti or other would feel the need at least every hour. The children didn't go for this much, since a meeting usually became necessary just at the point when they needed clean clothes, juice, a hug, or someone to play with and so on. That's where I came in. There are not a lot of jobs you can get without a work permit, being a Registered Alien like me. It took a few days for the butis to decide to employ me, since I clearly was not about to join the Community, but I kept coming back and mucking in and it just sort of happened.

Jan cleans up at the Community from seven to ten. How that happened was that Darren, the apple of her grandmotherly eye, was kicked out of the Rainbow Crèche for spitting and *language*, so she dragged him all over till she found the butis. I think the Rainbow people had rung everyone else to warn them. Jan has no opinion of her daughter May as a mother, and besides, she's decided May should have a career, since she never had the chance herself. She arrived with Darren in the middle of a meeting. It was probably the shortest meeting they ever had. Darren is two foot six of crew-cut aggro, and Jan won't hear a word against him. Can he help what git his mum decided to marry? 'Course he can't. He was a reason for a whole other meeting and they decided to accept him into their harmony. Then Jan refused to leave him unless the place got cleaned up. By eleven that morning she had installed herself as the cleaning dragon and there were twenty-seven earthenware bowls soaking in a strong solution of bleach. The butis accepted this new Inevitable with seraphic smiles.

Jan's main grouches were these:

How can you be healthy without meat?

What sort of men go round in brown sacks?

What do the booties find to smile about all day, like a bunch of half wits?

Even gallons of Dettol can't mask celestial incense, and try as she might, there was incense all over the floor every bleeding morning.

But Jan said it was better working than sitting at home watching the dust settle, even if it *was* working with a bunch of loonies. And it meant she could stand up for Darren, who showed no sign of needing anything but his hard little fists and a certain way with words.

There were a lot of other grouches too. Like what's the bleeding difference between fag smoke and josh sticks, eh? I go along with that one, and we'd commandeered the scullery back of the kitchen to *pollute our bodies with addictive anti-stress-related poison*. I swear the butis meditated about that, too. Jan could get fierce about cigarettes, she'd always smoked and it was her pleasure, she told the butis. Peace on you, sister. Jan smoked Number 10, and I smoke Samson which, as Jan says, is not a lady's cigarette. But then, I'm not a lady, am I? No offence, Jan says, and none taken, say I.

It's not really surprising that she saved up all the maggots for me to look at, at least once a week. The butis would no doubt bless them and see them a part of the divine process. They would certainly not approve of the various purges devised by Jan.

'I mean,' she spat out through her cigarette, 'I know maggots, you would do with the life I've had and the Pig I was married to. But what do you do? I've done bleach and Dettol and salt and vinegar, I even tried burning the buggers out. It's that back yard. It don't get done without it's me what does it, and I can't do it every day with them buggers throwing stuff all over the carpet. Look at it!'

She thrust the dustpan at me. Sure enough, maggots. This time they were a sickly blue-yellow and bigger than the last invasion, when they were red.

'I reckon they're getting used to what I put down. Probably think of bleach as a nice drink now. Maybe that's what's turned them white.'

She stared at me.

'Gawd help us all, look at the state of you! No need to ask who's been on the piss all weekend, and not for the first time. That bloke of yours playing you up, is he?'

I made the mistake of letting Jan know I share a flat with a Man. In Jan's book, you are either Engaged, Married, Divorced or Abandoned. I had to say something. But since then, she's leapt to all the wrong conclusions. Was he the drinking kind? Well, my flatmate Cherry drinks like a fish, but then, so do I. Maybe he was the type to go to clubs, then. Again, yes, but not the sort of clubs that she had in mind. Finally I said he was an actor. She seized on that with triumph and called him That Theatrical Type. In Jan's book, all men are Bastards and some worse than others, and the one she was married to found it hard to walk on his hind legs. She adored shopping for bargains and street markets and would have got on well with Cherry. And one of his wigs was just like her hair — rows of peroxide curls rigid with lacquer. He loved the sound of her and was always on at me to have her round for tea. In fact, he'd made a real scene about it yesterday. I never brought anyone home, he accused me, and he wanted to know why. I hadn't got the nerve to tell him I hadn't got the nerve.

'No, Jan, he's not playing me up.'

I couldn't class Sunday morning's action replay of Saturday night as 'playing me up'. Cherry had floated home at five, having wowed them at Shuff's and danced all night. A night of champagne where every man in the room looked like James Dean and Cherry was in his favourite spot: the centre of attention. No point in going to bed, dear, he trilled, I thought you'd like a cup of tea.

At six-thirty on Sunday morning? Is there a six-thirty on Sunday morning? I hadn't seen it before, and I wouldn't recommend it.

Jan was briskly maternal, having decided that I had been Wronged.

'Let's have a cup of tea, that'll wash it through you. Them little bleeders'll be here any moment now.'

The first cigarette of the day is a test of human endurance. Jan starts hers at four, for which I take my hat off to her. It is to be smoked, brain swimming, in silence. Jan slopped two tea bags into the bin and scooped sugar into her cup.

But oh, the second cigarette is bliss beyond telling!

'Now, let's see. Darren's having a kip out the back, poor little sod. His father was Out this weekend, so she sent him up my place. He's been with his granny all weekend,' she said with pride.

His father has no name as far as I know. He's That One, Mr Body Beautiful, I don't think, and the worst thing that's ever happened in Jan's family since her own husband.

'Mum was on the phone Sunday. Thinks she'll come up for a break. Won't be a break for me, I can tell you.'

Jan's mum has acquired the status of a legend. I can't imagine anyone intimidating Jan, but she swears she only married to get away from her. And Mum Knows Best, so when the Pig went off with its Tart, she told Jan never mind, dear, there's always people making a mess somewhere, you can always clean it up. And she does. City offices five to six-thirty, then the Community till ten. Ten-thirty to three she's at The World Turned Inside Out, daring the clientele to muck up her clean floor. Then she has Darren until May picks him up at seven. It's no life, her life, she says, but laughs with it.

The wind-chimes clattered in the passage.

Jan looked at her watch.

'Five to bleeding eight, I ask you. That'll be Omar. He's always first. I said to the booties, you ought to open at eight-thirty, but oh no, we are always open, he said. Open all hours.'

There was a rustle in the corridor. It is not for Jan or I to welcome people to the Community, although we do everything else. Little Omar burst into the kitchen, scarlet cheeks and runny nose.

'Dan! Doddyda, Dan!'

Jan picked him up and wiped his nose. What she says and what she does are two different things as far as children go. Bleeders, buggers and sods they may be before they arrive but, once they're there, it's her lap that they always land on.

'Ain't had no breakfast have you, you little mucker, eh?' she crooned. Omar always has cornflakes with us, the butis sigh angelically over the unblessed food, but it pleases Omar. And one rustle of the packet wakes Darren from the deepest sleep. So we sat feeling mellow while two little boys slurped into their bowls and giggled. Darren had that Monday morning look. He's got holy terror written all over his face, and his eyes are bursting with pure demon. When he smiles, you expect fangs, and there they are, rows and rows of sharp white teeth.

'Good morning to you, Jan and Monica. A beautiful day.'

Thus spake buti Agnetha. Every day is beautiful to the Community, regardless of what is happening outside. We smiled, it was hard to resist the sunrise glow of peace on Agnetha's face. But she looked grave when she noticed Omar and Darren and the cornflakes. Usually, you can rely on the butis meeting or meditating until nine or so.

'Do they like this *food*?' she asked, with buti superiority/humility — it could be either.

'I brought my May up on cornflakes,' said Jan warningly.

Agnetha nodded.

'It is not living food, is it, Jan?' she said sweetly.

'Well, I don't know about that. It's got nuts in.'

'And white sugar, Jan? Monica? *White* sugar?'

Honestly, you'd have thought we were trying to poison the children.

'Let them have honey. It will be better.'

Agnetha drifted serenely out of the kitchen.

'Right,' said Jan, rising swiftly. 'Never let it be said! Living food? Worms and bloody maggots, I suppose!'

Of course, by now, there was not much left in the way of cornflakes. But Jan dolloped out a huge spoon of honey into each plate and said to Darren: 'Eat your honey, darling, Granny's been poisoning you, hasn't she, and your mother as well?'

She said it in her licence to kill voice, and Darren's pale eyebrows wrinkled up towards her. I'm sure it was Jan egging him on that got him expelled from the Rainbow Crèche. God knows what they'd done to offend her. She has a rapport with her grandson, usually a reign of threatened terror, but he knows when he can let rip. This time, she shrugged and sat back. He scraped a little honey into his spoon and looked at her. She blew smoke serenely as he flicked it at the wall. And at the floor. And at Omar.

'I don't have nothing against honey,' she explained, 'but I ain't being told what to feed my own grandson.'

Omar got the idea pretty fast, only he used his fists. Honey spreads better that way. Between them they made a honey abstract on the beige walls, then, with a screech and a giggle, wriggled off their chairs to create chaos in the playroom.

'Wash your hands, Darren. And you, Omar.'

Jan nodded at me.

'Agnetha!'

They must have heard her a block away.

'They don't seem to like honey, Agnetha,' she said. If I didn't know, I'd have thought she was really worried. And buti Agnetha shook her head. Another manifestation of our unnatural times.

'Nevertheless, Jan, let us persist. It will be better. Oh, the waste of goodness . . .'

'I feel a meeting coming on,' said Jan, as she wiped the wall. 'Never mind, eh, keeps them out of our way.'

By nine, the playroom was like something censored out of *Gremlins*, and I spent most of the morning as a cross between Mummy Bear and Mister Wolf. I'd just been pinned to the floor, it was like an insane asylum in Lilliput, when buti Sikita beckoned me to the phone. Who in the hell would be ringing me at work?

'Oh hello, dear, were you busy?'

Cherry. I jammed one finger in my ear against the fourth circle of hell that had just broken loose.

'Look dear, Joe's just been up with a tray of sumptuous goodies. I was in the bath! He wouldn't look at me, said it was against his religion. I didn't like to accept, but you're having your Mrs Thing to tea today, aren't you, and I just wanted to say don't bother buying anything.'

'Cherry, I don't think . . .'

I was trying to fend off Wayne and Louise, playing Rambo with my knees. It was not the time to talk.

'I knew you'd be pleased. I shall be expecting you both! 'Bye!'

'But —'

But nothing. Madame Cherry had hung up, and if she was expecting us, we should come. It was not worth the sulk and you're ashamed of me aren't you that he could keep up for three days when required. I have never needed to watch Joan Crawford for much more than three hours.

'Jan, do you want to come to tea?'

This I shouted over morning watering-time, while our tiny charges discovered a hundred and one ways with pure organic apple juice. I was relieved to see her look doubtful.

'Well, I'd have to bring Darren. But he's no bother. Yes, that'd be lovely. I never had you down as the afternoon tea type, Monica. No offence, eh?'

Darren I'd forgotten about. I don't know how.

'No offence, Jan,' I said.

Yet.

'It's a lot of stairs, isn't it? Stop that, Darren.'

I turned the key in the lock. This could be the end of a friendship, one way or the other. What's that song — *every way you look at it, you lose*? If I hadn't brought Jan, Cherry would have sulked. Perish the thought. Now that I'd brought Jan, Cherry's sulks might be the least of it.

'Hi!' I called breezily. I am not a breezy sort of person, and I never say Hi.

The living room was as pristine as I'd ever seen it. So far, so good. Jan sat on one of our original moquette chairs and Darren picked up the atmosphere and, for the first time since I'd met him, sat on a chair in silence.

'Good afternoon.' The voice was contralto.

I had never seen Cherry in a suit before. Not one that involved trousers. He had only the slightest touch of rouge and a little mascara, which made him look healthy. But the effect was slightly marred by stilettos. Of course, he hadn't got any other shoes. Maybe Jan wouldn't notice. And maybe the Pope will start selling condoms.

'You must be Jan. But you look so young!'

'Well, I don't know what Monica's said.'

Full marks to Cherry, and less than zero to me. He was pure boy-next-door. A little fluttery, but positively macho beside the Queen of the Frocks I knew so well.

'I'm Basil, Monica's friend. And you must be Darren. How nice.'

Basil? And he hated children! Of course, it was Basil Rathbone, and just enough of a pause before 'friend' for Jan to think what she liked to think.

'Sit down, Monica, you must be exhausted!' He winked at me as he did a Gary Cooper out of the room. Well, well.

I was just beginning to stop sweating when Jan leaned over

and whispered: 'Why didn't you tell me he was a nancy boy, dear? My heart bleeds for you!'

Nancy boy is not a term I like, nor, I guess, one to be applied to Cherry Morello. It's like calling a *bombe glacée* pudding.

'I didn't know what you'd think!'

'Nan, what you whispering for?' said Darren out loud. 'Who's that funny man? What's he got make-up on for? Is he a poofter?'

Out of the mouths of babes and suckers. Jan raised her hand to Darren, and he collapsed in the chair with a pout like Marilyn Monroe.

I was not aware that we had a tea trolley dating from 1930. Cherry/Basil pushed it in, laden with cakes, doilies, lace mats, bone china and God knows what else.

'You be mother,' he glinted at me.

Jesus Christ!

Well, Jan thought it was marvellous. The tea, the china, the rug, the chairs, the monster treasure-house, it was lovely, and when Cherry/Basil made with the medium dry sherry it was even better. So much so that Jan got quite giggly and started swapping bargain stories with him, and I was left with Darren. Once he had eaten and smeared two or three cakes round his face and all over the chair, he wanted to see round the place.

'Show us your house, Monica,' he chanted, 'show us your house.'

He plonked himself in front of Cherry's Hollywood mirror and demanded to be made up like Boy George. I did my best.

'For God's sake!' shrilled Jan and her palsy-walsy Basil/ Cherry, who was not aware of the rising price on his head.

'Monica does try,' he simpered at Jan, 'but she's not really got the touch. Come here, Darren, let's do you properly.'

Darren trailed out after Cherry, gawping.

Jan licked sherry from her finger and leaned toward me. Why do people always want to give me maternal advice? The only person in my life with the natural right to do that, I had never met.

'No, love, you should have said he was a bit that way. God knows I'm not proud. My nephew, Martin, he's *one of them* and a lovely boy. He's got the same gift for furnishing as your Basil. Did my place up last year — you'd love it. I don't mind. It explains a lot,' said Jan, refilling the lustred bucket Cherry saw fit to drink sherry from. 'His mum wanted to chuck him out, but I said, he's your boy. Better being a poof than a Pig any day of the week.'

So now I was poor Monica, hung up on a nancy boy. I started working out a lingering death for Basil. Whose dulcet tones could be heard in the passage.

'Close your eyes, Nanna! Though I honestly thought you were his mum or his auntie, Jan! Now, open!'

I had to admit that I'd never seen Darren look so good. Somewhere, Cherry had dug out a gondolier's hat festooned with ribbons, and Darren's streetwise glower was masked by pouting lips and lyrical eyebrows. He had a Lurex shirt of Cherry's belted round him with a floral scarf, and his grin was like a piano keyboard.

'Oh, Basil! Don't he look a treat! Come to nanna, precious! Oh, isn't he a pet?'

I once had a book called *Enjoy Your Alligator*. And people do keep them as pets, I believe.

Well, this was a cue for music and more sherry, and I gave up as Boy Darren wiggled his hips, and *my Basil* and Jan swapped dressmaking hints. I escaped to the throne-room of James Dean. When I returned, Jan looked at me knowingly, as if darling Basil had told her about my embarrassing hump, third leg and cocaine habit.

'You should have said you were *that way*, Monica,' said Jan. 'I've been dead worried about you, it didn't seem right you not having a fella and liking children and all. I mean, I thought you

Recession

· ·

For Rae, every picture was a journey. The uncharted expanse of white was daunting and by way of preparation, she ruled squares on the canvas. She marked the meridians, numbered the latitudes and longitudes, and added a curlicue of compass points to make it navigable.

She'd started the picture in late summer, when sunlight scorched the dew from the grass a blink after rising, and she worked in shorts and a vest that said 'Beach Fun'. She had swathed meticulous leaves north-east to west-south-west, dotted in topaz and emerald, honey and olive.

There had been a week when she'd paced the studio humming or sat and gawped at the tapestry she'd created. It was perfect, like the letter-high illuminations in a medieval manuscript. For whimsy she'd even etched a skein of ants travelling due west, with a ladybird glowing like a winged jewel, poised to fly to her northern home. She wanted to throw a party on the ladybird day and made the mistake of wiping out a week's work with a red wine jag by way of celebration.

What had seemed so fresh and enticing at first was now stale, predictable. The viridescent mane of leaves seemed gaudy. Only to me, she told herself, as she cycled to the studio in the morning, no one else has taken these bearings, only I can shoot the sun this way. And even if someone from another age is standing on this spot, a ghostly paintbrush in her hand, her eyes wouldn't see what I see.

The words rang flat when she fastened back the shutters. Same damn bit of canvas, same damn picture. Days like this, she wished people would drop in for coffee, knowing they wouldn't after the song and dance she made about needing solitude. How did it go, that high-minded bit of soapbox? *If I had a nine-to-five job in an office, you couldn't just call in. It devalues me as an artist, painting is WORK, just because I'm a woman*. Etcetera.

She hadn't meant to drive them away completely. Equally, she couldn't expect them to be psychic and intuit when it was okay. To hell with reason, she was scared today: what if she'd lost her way, and nothing could put her on the right track.

I need some new music, she thought.

Part of the fellowship was the lease on the studio. She'd taken it because of its isolation, lost near a lake in the grounds of an old asylum. There was no phone. Winter days like today she imagined mad, anxious ghosts pacing the grass, walking through the naked trees, wailing at the misted water. Riding over the cattle grid, she heard chains rattling, and glanced at the high, barred windows in the empty Victorian pile built to house the mentally afflicted. In their zest for reform, the Victorians felt that madness was caused by the three Ws: worry, want and wickedness. They would transform madness to lunacy and cure it with the three Ms: method, meat and morality.

Rae felt jaded. It had happened before, she must just plot the next square like painting by numbers. Paint along with Nancy Kominsky time, she called it. She'd watched the TV programme once, when Nancy was 'doing' a cottage garden. 'You do a row of liddle white lines, not too regular, then you back up a row of liddle grey lines next to 'em. That's your fence.' The trouble was, she might be right.

Weeks later, she was still painting by numbers. There was a lake and a sweep of land blurring into mountains. She'd intended the pleasure-bound figures by the lake to be stylized and realised that they looked sinister, as if an architect's drawing was peopled by a sideshow of grotesques. Freaks. Perhaps because she'd dressed them for winter? One woman looked as if she was carrying ice-skates, and maybe that meant that the lake should be frozen. If it's summer from west-south-west to north-east, then where does winter lie?

A new moon lay in the clear blue sky. There were no shadows. And so what, she thought, so what? She'd tacked the first sketches for this picture up on the wall and they looked as if someone else had drawn them. Why on earth had she wanted an anthropomorphic chessboard effect on the hills? Everything jarred. The debris on the floor alarmed her: screwed-up paper, stale coffee-cups, heels of sandwiches. Usually, foot-high clutter meant a flurry of inspiration, but now it said, stalemate, you're stale, mate, you're stuck . . .

New music would help, but it meant going into town and choosing. What a terrible task, she mocked herself, how we artists suffer. And then there was money. Or rather, there wasn't. With the lease on the studio, the rent was peanuts and she'd paid it all up front from the last exhibition, congratulating herself on being so sensible. What the hell did she buy anyway, apart from tobacco, coffee, wine, canned soup, baked beans, canned spaghetti? She was perfectly happy to live like a student twenty years after art college, anything so long as she could paint.

Maybe that was why this picture just wouldn't work: she was expected to produce a suitable work in return for the fellowship that was supposed to be paying her just to paint. She'd decided on a plain pastoral view of the asylum and its grounds, it was supposed to be routine. She didn't want to paint the building — knowing her driving perfectionism, she'd spend weeks showing every brick. If she hadn't started with the leaves it would have been easy, irritatingly so. But with the leaves came disturbing choices: they promised a different view of lake, tree, asylum and hills. A new sound in the air could take her there, it was a longed-for and prayed-for wind lifting the sails of a ship in the doldrums. Tough. No new music until the next cheque.

Rae rifled through the jumble of cassettes and hauled out seven unmarked possibilities. Number one was Bob Dylan and she cut it off after the first sneering words of despair. Number two was static and reggae, pirated from the pirate station DBC years before in Paddington. Marianne Faithfull, Marlene Dietrich, tragedy and camp. Then the third and last cassette yielded Mozart and she smiled.

Poor old Wolfgang, she thought, and I think I've got money troubles. How did he manage to juggle all the instruments and conjure sounds no one has matched? All around him, back-stabbing and financial disaster fomented chaos, inside he had discovered a universe of beauty and order. Mozart always sounded effortless, fresh as paint. She tipped the cassette box out on the floor and jumbled them all back: what she'd not heard for ages was now at the top. The surprise of the old would have to do.

The only bit of the picture she was sure of was the leaves, the outline of the hills and the brand new moon. She hadn't wanted to have people at all, but there they were and what was she to do with them? At a stroke she could make them vanish, but she'd still see them. She opened the French doors and leaned there, looking at the lake.

In the gloom, she pictured the sad, mad people who'd walked there. Each one would have had an attendant to stop them doing themself harm. They might have been in the private wing, put away by their guilty and embarrassed families. Would they have tried to escape?

Once, years before, she'd visited her friend Julie in a psychiatric unit and it struck her that a lot of the people wanted to be there. Reality had become nightmare for them and they'd opted out into a world where meals came, drugs were given, and all the doors were locked except for the bathroom. Julie had said, quite matter-of-fact: 'I pissed myself yesterday.'

A young man in Jesus sandals walked past shouting 'FUCK FUCK FUCK FUCK.' A woman was rocking in a corner. Another woman stood on one leg by the window and stared at her. The nurses sat in the glass-screened office, gossiping. She watched her friend's institutional baby-blue smock turn dark along her thighs.

Months later, Julie came out and talked about it.

'You know when I pissed myself, Rae, well, it was okay. You expect to be told off and you're not. So I did it a lot. I couldn't be bothered to go to the toilet and they always came and changed me. Then I stopped, you know why?'

'Tell me,' said Rae.

'The doctor said I'd get sores and they'd hurt. I hadn't thought of that. I didn't want to get sores. I stopped.'

And the woman in her picture, with her Victorian gown: had she pissed herself and calmly waited to be changed? Rae closed her eyes. She'd often been accused of impersonality in her work and it was the criticism that stung her most. Another rant: *if I slop paint everywhere, I've got feelings. When I observe and use skill, I'm cold. Why does everyone think emotion has to be messy?* In a fit of pique, she'd included some wild canvases in the last show. *Untitled 1, Untitled 2, Untitled 3*. They hadn't sold, they were the work of an undisciplined talent, so the critics said. Untitled, undisciplined — well, Mozart I ain't, she thought.

One day, she was cycling in just after dawn and the winter grey had lifted on an ice-blue horizon. She stopped at the bridge over the estuary and watched the sea birds swoop over mud, chocolate-brown with slabs of black sheen like coal. The tide was out and pools of water trapped the sky like shattered mirrors. The light was enough after misty moisty months of grey: spring would not be long. She rode furiously to the asylum grounds and looked up at the tree where the leaves had run riot in late summer. It was the tallest tree, and June and July saw its waxy flowers bold as a candelabra. A horse chestnut. The trunk was studded with knot-holes spaced for climbing and the naked branches spun upwards as evenly as the treads of a spiral staircase.

She started Mozart with the press of a button and kept on her fingerless gloves against the cold. She painted a woman in the tree, just her head and shoulders with one arm reaching through the leaves for balance. She had a childish face and her other arm was raised, her hand stretched as if beckoning or about to smother a giggle. She made the mischievous eyes look at her and one finger pointed at the ladybird, another drew her gaze downwards to the lake. This woman would be the one in the attic, the one nobody paid for, the one they fed because they had to and treated like filth because she didn't seem to notice or care. She'd be left sitting in a pool of piss until they couldn't stand the smell. She'd be punished.

In those days, she might have been no more mad than to fall for a handsome stranger and carry his child. Abandoned to drink from her cup of sorrow, the asylum superintendents would have marked the baby as 'an accidental addition which wholly unbalances the tottering mind'. The lofty reformers had cast away the restraints of the bedlam years: gyves and muzzles and scold's bridles, fetters and hobbles and manacles. She would be recorded as one of the 'morally insane'. A woman who had never held her own child or even seen it. Whose womb would be forever empty, whose heart would scream. A woman who would never walk free in the sunshine, serving a life-sentence where today child murderers are punished by countable years or even months. A woman driven over the edge. Hysterical, demented, deluded. The madwoman in the attic. In a padlocked world of her own, up the pole, off her rocker, out of her tree.

Trapped and mad as the birds, she'd have seen the horse chestnut and its thick green kaleidoscope of leaves from her barred window. She'd have watched through the seasons — how many Novembers, how many Junes? — and noted the easy stairwell of living wood, raggy in autumn, then winter-bare and ridged with snow. Maybe. Somewhere and somehow she'd given them the slip, shinned down the mat of Virginia creeper in the darkness and scuttled across the lawn to hide. Maybe. More likely she just ran into the tree and panicked as the sun threatened to rise like a spotlight and expose her. Rae imagined the fear in her sunless face as she scrambled up the rough bark. Now she was safely east-north-east in her green canopy, her pale lips laughing at them all. Summertime, one day when her living was easy.

Rae was up before dawn all that week. Evenings she came home to a stack of manila envelopes with folded papers lettered in scarlet and black. She'd ignored them long enough, glaring at their dusty little windows on the bottom stair as she came in and left. Fly away Peter, fly away Paul? No chance, they'd brought their bureaucratically extended families to stay. She scooped them up and dumped them on the table.

'Can't make it this evening,' she told her friends in a phone call, 'I'm clearing my desk. Paperwork, dahlinks, it comes to us all.'

She sent off cheques with no date, cheques she hadn't signed, letters with minor queries, letters without cheques. All she had to do was hold them at bay for a few weeks. She had crossed this road before, deftly robbing Peter to slip a rubber cheque into Paul's back pocket. March wasn't that far away.

She tarted up her grey-black sweatshirt and her grey-black jeans with a belt from the neanderthal squalor of the bottom of the wardrobe. She even tarted up the buckle with sequins and pinned feathers in her battered hat. Might as well look the part, since all artists were considered crazy and bohemian. When she got on her bike, she was a highwaywoman on a ramshackle steed. In the paper shop, she bought tobacco.

'Daylight robbery these days,' said the customer ahead of her. 'When's it going to end?'

She thought of the days when art was a rich man's pastime and voluptuous whores took the back stairs to Burne-Jones' studio to be recreated in the image of Cleopatra for tuppence ha'penny an hour. Without inherited wealth or a rich patron, you couldn't dream of painting. But she'd been born at a better time and there were arts councils and they had been good to her. Forget not good enough, she was still eating and drinking and her flat was usually warm. It was not bad for the time of year: February was always her cruellest month.

She was working so well that her coffee was always cold before she remembered to drink it. She'd flooded the picture, drowning the little people, and the waters of the lake lapped the edge of the canvas. She repainted the figures in the foreground, each button and strand of hair etched with photographic precision. The attendants were a uniform dun and grey, steel rings of keys at their waists. Their mad charges wore bright colours like children. The lady in the candy-pink dress still carried her ice-skates and the boots were soft white kid, the sun flashing on the blades.

On the first day of March, her cheque arrived and she bought a bright green T-shirt to celebrate. That was the day she saw the first crocuses around the roots of the tree. She stole their golden hearts and gave the lakeside people garlands, linking their stilted arms like dancers. There were lambs to put on the hillsides and dragonflies swooped the surface of the lake, clear and still from east to west-sou'-west. Was it finished? She hardly dared look.

She cleared the studio floor into a black plastic bag and boiled water for the cups with their ridged contour lines of coffee. She swept dust out of the open doors and stood her brushes in glass jars of turps along the windowsill. It was time for a studio party. Damned if the foundation could have this picture; she'd give them the nameless three condemned as undisciplined talent. Rae was going to break her golden rule and hang this one in her own living room. She wanted to call it something, as well — how about *The Twilight Season*? Crap. The madwoman in the tree was the only creature of winter and she was bright-eyed as the ladybird. Yes, it was complete. Rae scratched her initials due south-west and turned the easel to face the door. Sitting and looking at it, she nodded: she'd call it *Fly Away Home*.

Kids' Stuff

· ·

May walked home from school with her fingers spread like a beached starfish. If the wind blew on the edge of her hand there would be trouble. It sneaked up through her coat buttons, ballooned her sleeves and stung her face. The days she met the wind full on, something awful happened as soon as she got home. Those days she walked slowly, crying already and biting and snuffing back the tears. At the end of her street, she'd run in a mad panic, pelting round to the back door. It could be late she'd get wrong for.

Sometimes the slaps were delivered with a smile, sometimes after a scream, sometimes in silence, sometimes in the middle of the screaming. If she answered back, woe betide her. If she kept mum, God help her. An open palm, a fist, a stick, a belt, a saucepan: whatever came to hand. Nothing was right with the wind full on.

When the wind blew through her fingers she'd be all right. It pinned her sleeves to her side and cuffed both cheeks; somehow it blew all the badness away and out of her and she was safe.

Her mam would be singing with tea on the table. Maybe her auntie would be there. Or the next-door neighbour. Someone to stop the madness and the beating. Something good always happened with the wind skew-whiff.

Her friend Izzy said, Why d'you do that, you look barmy walking like a robot, look at you.

She said, Well, Izzy busybody, you go doo-lally tap if you put half a toe on a crack in the pavement, I've seen you. What do you do *that* for?

A crack on the pavement meant another night when her dad would come in roaring drunk and roaring them all in and out of bed all night to say the catechism. And the belt buckle for every word wrong. Her mam would say nothing, just sit there white-faced, cupping her hand over the latest bruise, not daring even to blink in case he said she was sleeping in God's time when all he wanted was to raise his children decent. You had to be careful walking home, not walk like a zombie, sticking your arms out with your fingers like a baby stretching out for a dropped dummy.

I've got my reasons, said Izzy.

May never had to bother about the wind on a Friday. Fridays she went to her nanna's and the wind could blow away the chimneypots without having the slightest effect on her nanna. Once she shut the door of her house, everything was fine inside. It was warm in the winter with the coals making fiery caves and purple tunnels for magic stories. It was cool and fresh in the summer, the back yard blooming with wallflowers and purple bells. There was just enough sunshine to play in and just enough shade to lie in, reading while Nana sat and darned.

But today was Monday, the first and the worst day, getting used to the maverick wind, going as slow as possible up to the corner where she had to say goodbye to Izzy and face it all alone.

Look at *her*, May jeered, nodding over the road, thinks she's a ballet dancer. Satin slippers to school!

Her dad's got a car, said Izzy.

I'm getting a car as soon as I'm sixteen. My dad told me.

And I'm the Empress of China!

I am though, said May, and I'm going to drive it everywhere. Her dad's got one already. And she gets piano lessons.

Over the road, Jessica Haddow was making herself invisible. If she walked lightly, light as a feather, breathing like a sparrow, she'd turn to thistledown and just drift in a window at home. Be in bed before they saw her. Mummy said she was a good girl when she was asleep. Of course, if there were cars in the street outside her house, it would be lovely. Mummy would have Mrs Thing bring in a trolley with cakes and sandwiches and tell her to play the piano for the Guests. She'd slip away to the kitchen for tea and be washed and in her nightclothes for seven, just long enough to kiss her daddy goodnight. She'd smell the pipe and the sherry in the lounge and know she could go to sleep, because the Guests would be staying for supper and cards. Daddy never shouted while they were there. Mummy never cried.

It was all right for the likes of May and Izzy, always shouting and laughing and making her cry. Taking all her words and throwing them back at her in silly high voices. She didn't sound like that — did she?

Jessica skipped and prayed and crossed her fingers. Mummy would be crying if she was alone and as soon as Daddy's key turned in the lock, it would be her fault. Even if she'd dabbed Mummy's eyes and wiped her brow with a hanky soaked in cologne. She'd be sent to her room and hear them going on about how if it wasn't for The Child — her — everything would be different and it would have ended years ago. Two voices, one cross and booming, one bitter and high, through her bedroom floor, up the stairs, under her door, even through her pillow. On and on and on.

Dear God, let there be Guests, prayed Jessica, or let Daddy be away on business.

That didn't happen very often, maybe three times a year, maybe a week at a time. But Mummy opened all the drapes and smiled and laughed when he was away. They had picnics in the garden, and played cards way past her bedtime. She even got a goodnight story and kiss when Daddy was away.

But then she stopped. If she wished him away then he might die and it would be her fault. Dear God, thought Jessica, seeing the words in her best handwriting, Dear God let it be all right when I get home and I'll never. . .

She faltered. Never what? What could she bargain with? What could she give God for a sacrifice? Miss Arabella Marks, said her mind, cold and clear. Surely not that, she thought, my best doll, she's got real hair and blue eyes that open and shut eyelashes and says Mama. *Bury Miss Arabella Marks in the garden*, said her mind. Jessica sat on a wall, her nose pink with cold and crying. No! Not *I'll never*. Dear God, make everything all right and I'll always be nice to people, even May and Izzy. She ran home, ran as fast as she could; she was running from the picture of Miss Arabella Marks deep in a hole where earth crept up round her lace-frilled socks and drowned her beautiful blue eyes.

Alice dawdled in the playground. She'd been wanting to go home all day, dragging on her teacher's hand on the way in, looking over her shoulder just in case her mum might have popped her head round the gate for a last wave.

Mustn't be late home, said her teacher, off you pop.

She turned left out of the playground. It was the long way round, but she did it every day. It was necessary. That way *They* couldn't follow her home. She dived down the first alleyway, until she came to the window beside the white door with the red strip on the step. In the window there was a magic ship inside a bottle. It sailed a sea painted sky-blue and there was even a figure with eyes and a mouth in a crow's-nest smaller than an acorn. On either side of the magic ship-in-a-bottle stood two grey-lustred vases with gold flowers on the side and big bunches of pink roses all year round.

Good. There were no footsteps behind her.

Further down the alleyway the wood had shrunk in a fence leaving a knot-hole big enough to see through. She peered at the tangle of brambles inside and shook with excitement: there was a perfect spider's web today. Luck or money — either was welcome. She ran to the next corner with her head down, past the boarded-up house and the gate where a dog's nose pushed under a loose board. The corner house had yellow curtains upstairs. Today they were open and the glass was a bare blank.

Oh dear. They might already have seen her.

She'd have to go down the muddy lane now. Here, in a series of wrecked sheds, men mended cars or sat on old tyres, smoking. Their dogs looked like wolves who'd scoured a coal tip and sometimes they barked and the men shouted. Probably at her. She didn't know. Today they were busy and the dogs were chained, so it didn't matter so much about the naked window. Maybe.

Then came the road where her knees went funny. She could either step off the pavement or walk with a clang on an iron hatch she was sure would cave in one day and she'd be deep underground and lost forever. That was where the draymen rolled great steel barrels, and it was held up only by bolts. She'd seen them! Worse, every house had a grating below the window, where straggling plants clung to dripping black earth. Most of the gratings were painted black, but some were skinny with rust.

She knew she was late when the blue door was closed. Usually an old woman sat there, patting a matted dog with blind eyes. Alice had to breathe really hard not to cross the road there, for although the old woman always smiled, the hallway behind her was dark brown and went on forever.

Marigold bonfire railings house was three streets from home. No one seemed to live there. The grass was wild and ragged with dandelions, and a charred pile of board blocked the path. But pressed up against the railings there were waxy gold marigolds, sunshine yellow flowers, bronze floppy heads and one clump almost the colour of blood.

Craven Terrace had lost its C, and she scurried along fearing the steel-black swoop of huge birds plucking her high into the air to drop her like a snail and scoop up the pulp.

She flattened herself against the end terrace wall and looked back. No one. She'd shaken them off. It was safe to walk down her street.

Four houses from home lived an old lady who no one saw. Her mother said she'd fallen on hard times. From her front door to the wall was a room made of glass with royal-blue diamonds next to the collapsed guttering. Her garden was full of poppies and Alice snatched two of the hairy buds as she went by. Hen or cockerel? Hen or cockerel? She shut her eyes and boldly said hen and hen.

A miracle! Hen meant pink silky petals, cockerel was squashed scarlet. Everything was going to be fine. She flung both pink buds over her shoulder and ran into the back kitchen shouting, Mam, mam, I'm here!

Her mam was cutting bread and shook her head.

That's a bit loud, isn't it? she said. Wash your face and hands.

She didn't know that Alice had saved her, yet again. *They* wouldn't be knocking at the door tonight, nor any other night so long as she was careful. Mam would never guess how brave she had been all the way home. And she need never know.

Fugue

· ·

Breakfast time. Muesli and coffee, papers delivered. I looked up and saw only an outline where he was sitting. I could see straight through him to the muddy, catpaw marks on the back door.

There was a hum in the air like radio static; I took it to be his voice, and I made answers when the static paused.

Quack.

Oh, QUACK!

Quack, quack, quack.

Nothing in the sing-song drone showed that he noticed. Then his outline moved upright, a jarring elastic shape like cartoon smoke gone mad. It hovered close to me and I felt a coldness on my cheek. More humming, exasperation at locating the briefcase, hat and furled umbrella, and the front door made a closing sound.

He was gone.

Gone to work and see-you-later-dear. The clock said seven. Forty. Five. Five minutes to the train.

I went to wash up as the table edge trembled to a familiar sick-to-the-gut miasma of nothingness. Water came from the taps and sat in an unnerving basin shape: the blue plastic failed to dematerialise from the world where I had been a grateful and temporary guest since the moment five years ago when I had vouchsafed in the sight of the God of men *I do*. As I placed them in the water, the bone-china cups and saucers became first glass then nothing; the water was cold as a glacier. The bubbles of foam trembled to mist and I sensed the house become dangerous, a mirage to my eyes. While I could still feel and just see it, I opened the back door to the garden.

I left it open.

Last time I had been a fool enough to close French doors and knew they were there only frantic moments later, when I saw blood spatter my wrists and hands, like a fly buzzing, like a bird beating against the see-through reality. I knew to leave the door open, as I knew to clear a path to the kitchen door, while the chairs were still hand-stripped pine to me.

The garden was there. No garden chairs, of course. We had put them out only last week, in hopes of May meaning spring was here. And the rosebush culled from the best North-West London nursery — he'd planted it last Saturday — was only there for me when I ripped scarlet beads of blood from thin air.

I sat on solid ground, my back against a tree.

I should have known. All the signs were there.

It started at that triumphant dinner party last Thursday. He had landed a contract as pleased as Punch, and I made a feast for his friends. *That's the way to do it!* The air dissolved around cordon bleu, and all I heard were parrot screeches, barking and the blowing of a horse's soft mouth — that was him — and all I could say was: *Quack, quack, quack.* It lasted only minutes by the clock and I thought, perhaps, I was over-tired. The last doctor had warned me against a relapse before he set me free. But five years! Five years with *him*, my love, my dove, my one and truly — I'd had the nerve to consider myself cured, paroled, out on good behaviour. And it had been so good!

I lit a cigarette. *He* hates it and doesn't know what it means to me. The white tube, the cork-effect filter, the solid hot flare of the match and my lips tell me of my lungs as I make my own smoke, with its blue drifting and acrid smell.

What if *he* came in this evening through a door that wasn't there and sat in a chair-shape, reading a paper that had never been printed, saying aloud bits that were only hum and haw again to me? Just how long would quack, quack last before he knew?

In my heart, I knew what I must do. But so many times before I had done just this thing, been reviled as a mind-fucking bitch with a heart of stone. I loved him, as much as an alien can entertain love for a being on a green planet where she knows she has only a certain time.

He was the one who had been inside me, so that I suddenly knew, like a reprieve, a baby was coming, my links were strengthening. And when the bud grew in me, and I knew her every cell as it pulsed to life; when I felt the pliant fingernails and rip of flesh that is a mouth: then I knew this was *my* planet. I'd beaten it! I was here! Such a short time she was in my arms and then we had to find a hole in the earth to place her; a piece of stone to mark her passing. He was so kind, remained solid flesh and blood around me, made a solid shape against the trembling anguish calling itself mother. Dead mother of a dead baby.

Better luck next time ... but the doctor told me there would be no next time.

He made rainbows for me, parties and different clothes and the terrifying miasma of wine when the room became an architect's outline of people in a building made of lines and shadows.

Water with the wine.

We managed.

The garden palled into coldness. It was time to gird up my loins, the way the black skirts and white garotte of the preacher's collar had boomed when my grandmother-who-was-not had taken me by the hand to church so many times.

Careless talk costs lives.

I was a war baby and a shame to my birth-dead mother who had given herself to the last-time-leave blandishments of my faceless father. Granny, they said, was a good Christian woman, though I knew like a flame burns true that she was perfect with no riders, the empress of her acres, her livestock. She was solid, warm, and there for me, right till the day she died. But it had started when I was still with her.

Post-war euphoria, when the Big House ransacked its rose-garden and all the village wore roses. We sailed down the High Street to Butcher Tom's. No more ounces of liver for those who saved their stamps! Granny was a galleon in the queue of *our boys*, glowing and clucking. Then we were by the counter and through the glass I saw a feathered corpse, twisted to show its plumpness. The head of a duck sat meek on the neck of a duck, beak sleek in her breast feathers.

Butcher Tom picked her up, and I could see that her neck was broken. He chopped, and her eyes fixed on me, bead-black and ebony-shining.

Quack. Quack.

Her severed head flopped on a bin of guts, yellow beak in a grimace — take me with you?

Granny plucked her and stuffed her and basted her and served her to the table, golden and gleaming. The war was over. And I ate her flesh, nearly sick on every rich mouthful, stuffing myself full after years of soup, gnawed carrots and turnips. In the afternoon, we took crusts, finally acknowledged as too stale even for puddings, to throw on the waters and the live ducks dived greedily, a raucous caucus, batting aside moorhens and dabchicks, and Granny said:

'*V-Day. Remember this day, child.*'

I found her body chill in bed one morning. They called her *dead*.

Afterwards, she wasn't there any more. There was a stone in the windswept graveyard that bore her name, there were good times around the corner. Everybody said so, every day. The only corners I knew were in the playground where boys tried to fumble in my knickers, and street corners where the winds met head-on. No good times there. There was a woman who wanted me to call her mother, and then called me awkward, exasperated and frightened with the dreams and the screams. *I can't manage her, she doesn't seem to hear me.* And then a big house where the children were so many and we had one mother for all of us.

I remember, I remember
The house where I was born.
I don't. Granny used to sing the words to me while I fell asleep.

Then the first man came along, with talk of marriage.

Mother-of-so-many said: 'You're of an age and you could do worse. Here are your papers. Give them to your husband to take care of.'

I felt curious as I said the words in an office to a man the other side of a desk with white flowers and greenery in a vase. In the house next to where I lived with him was another married woman. I copied her, always one day behind, she washed on Monday, I washed on Tuesday. She had fish on Friday, salad on Saturday, roast on Sunday. It did us well enough, I thought, until the day he started shouting about a real wife, a real home, a Sunday roast and babies. As he talked, he faded into an outline and I found myself beating folded wings and saying, *Oh, quack, quack, quack, quack.* Then his smoke-outline blurred to darkness and it was a long time until I woke.

And then I was in bed, with sheets riveted over my body up to my chin. I could see through slitted eyes many people who had the comfort of being three-dimensional, walking and talking words that I knew. The sense was neither here nor there, but oh the words came easy and I breathed again and ate again. White blurs passed around us and coloured pills stuck in my throat but, from time to time, I saw a man in a room on my own and he always asked me how I was feeling. Thank God he didn't know what I was sure of, that I *felt* everything as if through a mattress. Whatever he heard me say, some time later I was led out of the doors and taken to rooms they said were mine, as if they were pleased about it.

I was required every day to go to another place and put cards coloured like the cooked liver of a duck into alphabetical order. I did it. They gave me money, and I put it into a jar like Granny had with the egg money. A woman would come from time to time and take my money and bring me clothes and food.

Then *he* came. And it was marriage again, only white and spring churchyard and hundreds of people smiling about it all. His mother, his father, his sisters, his brother.

'Now you're part of the family.'

They said it again and again.

All at once I was gusted along, and really felt: a heartbeat when I saw him, a warmth when he touched me; I smelt the flowers he bought me and the spicy perfume he put on his skin. I was alive like running in Granny's fields. And then the baby, and then not the baby, but there was an us I could feel to be there every day when I woke up.

The tree-bark nudged pain into my back. Nine o'clock the kitchen clock said. I found my way by memory up the stairs and pulled my case from the top of 'our' wardrobe. So many grey and shimmering dresses, suits, shirts and ties. This was my case, dusted down from Granny's attic when they were taking me away from the farm.

Take what you need, dear.

Granny was gone and I couldn't take her, try as I might. My best dress that she'd sewed, my blouses with her embroidery: I put them in the hard square leather case. They weren't there when I opened it. The new woman who wanted to be called mother put a stack of blouses and skirts out for me, like you might give milk to a stray cat.

What happened to the old grey goose?

The old grey goose is dead.

What happened to the scratching, yawning, barking dog?

What happened to the brown bowls where Granny put out water and corn and grain?

I have my leather case, hardly bigger than the case he takes to the office every day. I put it on the bed where we made the baby that wasn't and what am I to put in the water-marked, dog-tooth lining?

There is a blouse of midnight blue with a diamond flower that sat on my breast when I wore it. For the firm's dance. I liked the sound of that: firm. My husband works for a firm. But it was music and shapes trying to move with the music. And then there were skirts, make and match, sew-along-with-Nancy Liebowitz. The TV afternoons and the hours went so slow until he came back and turned the lights on.

I close the twin catches on the clothes. Just in time, for the bed where I placed the case is flashing its warning negative/ positive, and I snatch the stitched handle, just in time, as it fades out.

Now I know time is against me: the horror of being left thirteen feet in the air with no stairs to reach the ground! I walk down the real staircase, but I know, like Lot's wife knew, that everything is crumbling to a smoke screen behind me, the urge to look back slaps at my face, but there has been enough powder to nothing in my life. I clasp the mahogany handle just as the door shivers its infection and walk down the crazy paving path as each stone vaporises one step behind me.

'Good morning, duck, how are you today then?'

I froze when they first said that in the town where we lived for his firm job. *Hello, me duck, are you all right, ducks, I'm fair done in, ducks.*

But they never needed an answer, clucked after me that I was a poor thin thing and shy with it, but a lovely smile.

Me and my lovely smile walk down the street, the sky going dark grey, every lamp post vanishing with a crack of lightning as I pass it. Then the rain.

The ghost car shapes throw up real spray at me. I stand still, eyes closed, the cold blessed water on my face and neck, soaking into my shoes.

When my eyes open, I am out of town. I think. Perhaps the town has gone. It's hard to tell. My ankles are stroked hard by thick wet grass. It's a roadside somewhere — the same day? Or another day and place of rain. Who's to say?

A great silver shape comes out of the rain beside me. Lorry. Lift in lorry, going places, king of the road.

'You must be soaked!'

A tattooed arm reaches down from the high cab — lovely, real arm, wonderful words! — and I scale the high steps to sit with my feet on a coil of rope.

'Lovely weather for the ducks!'

His words come clear, and his face focuses, red, unshaven, a cigarette, little black shiny eyes, a smile.

'Have a fag.'

'Yes, please,' I say.

The relief of the match, the tube, the words. *Yes, please.* I said those words. I hear them as the smoke confirms me. I am back. For the time. Being.

Off Season

· ·

It was Tuesday evening and Frances was going dancing. She'd showered and lightened her hair, clipped gold in her ears and at her throat, slid into a renaissance shirt and pants of soft silk and called a cab. As she straightened up from tying her shoes, the pain struck. She dropped into the chair, whispering *No, not now, I've been so careful*. As if pleading helped — she might as well try to appeal to the better nature of a power-crazed tyrant. Shifting her arm stemmed it, but seconds later it burst through, an acid river ugly with shale blasting holes in her shoulder.

So, once again, I have to acknowledge pain. She spat the words. She was furious.

She could, of course, bang it on the head with painkillers. Stun it with one dose and swat it with the next. Knock it senseless every hour when it raised its fanged head and decided to sharpen its nasty little claws. But tonight she was going to Le Club Zodiaque, tonight she wanted to sip wine until her feet were flying. Painkillers and wine? A stupefying cocktail. Tonight was for chandeliers and the champagne genie who makes your brightest dreams come true.

Frances sighed. Patience, old thing, don't fight it. Forget justice. You have to go with it, riding the pain like a horse that flattens its ears and shies away from you.

She lit a cigarette and closed her eyes. Calm down. Keep your chin up. Know the beast and tame it.

She remembered a diagram in the biology text book: Transverse Section Through Human Skin. A cornified layer, a granular layer. The self-renewing Malphighian layer snaking around the dermis, dense as earth. Fat in round globules like pebbles, hair-roots like grass, capillary loops and sweat glands like worm tunnels. Little black nerve lines wriggling like streams. Flesh.

Her shoulder was an uneasy cloak of skin holding inside it her pain. Muscles: scarlet living meat tethered by milky-blue tendons to bones. In this tortured landscape, the shoulder blade was their anchor, bleached and bare as the river-smoothed head of a Neanderthal axe. A honeycomb of caves pulsed inside the bone. Each part was cushioned by synovial fluid. Nothing was ever still: even in deep sleep they shifted with every rise and fall of her automatic lungs. There was a whole ocean inside her and the tide rolled to the beat of her heart.

She tried to goad herself through the panic. So many years a teacher, you know it all! she sneered, feeling her face twist grey and cold. She shuddered and forced herself to breathe deep.

OK, teacher. Now tell me about pain.

Maybe there is a slight depression in a vein, just like a child standing on a hosepipe: water can't get through. The blood doesn't flow and so the muscle shrinks a little, its elastic tendons stretch to normalize. The stretch pulls the bone away from its perfect-fit socket — maybe just a millimetre. The whole shoulder lurches out of balance, registering danger.

It was like walking on flints with bare feet, and her raw bones corroded inside her. Alarm transmitted through an intricate tracery of nerves, each fibre twanged like a web hit by a fly. Red alert!

Frances experienced the red alert as agony.

Massage the skin and pass on the pressure and bingo! Vein unkinks, blood flows, muscle expands, tendons ease, shoulder bone snuggles back into place. All clear: sparks fly along the nerve wires, pins and needles and it's over. Stretch goodbye to the pain and forget you even have a shoulder. Normality.

But this rough-shod torment was no stranger. She'd known its cut and thrust on and off for years now. It mightn't be a vein. Anything could be off-beam. Suppose the tendon had stretched for so long it couldn't tauten, or the muscle was shrunk so dry its tiny capillaries were flat and empty. Suppose the smooth ball of bone had been held away from its snug socket just too long to glide easily back into place.

Inside Frances, the cushion of fluid was crystals, her bones ground together, their cartilage dry as rawhide; her veins were clogged and everything chafed and griped.

And how to clear the silted tunnels of their fluid debris, wash the stale blood away, consign this minor crucifixion to uneasy memory? The fingers of her other hand stretched and pressed, but the log jam was centred just out of reach. She'd read that when an elephant has a wound, the mahout squirts chilli juice in its eyes by way of distraction. She winced at the thought and concentrated on the toes of her right foot, those tireless weight-lifters and balancers, dusted with rose-scented powder and snuggled into rainbowed socks and patent leather shoes.

Everything was in order down there, twenty-something bones webbed and working wonders with never a twinge. Tarsals, metatarsals, phalanges, good evening, she thought, you shall go to the ball! As she arched her foot, her hand automatically flexed and a strand of hope flickered up her arm and across her back. The pain sheathed its claws. She drummed her fingers and each beat whiplashed it a little further back, snarling, but at bay.

She eased on her jacket when the taxi came and sprawled on

the back seat, watching the garlands of Christmas lights slung across the streets. Waterfalls of white and gold, shooting stars in scarlet and yellow, Christmas trees shimmering as if touched by fairy wands.

The hotel lobby was a fantasia of streamers and lanterns. Music piped from nowhere and everywhere with the dream of a white Christmas. The solemn lift operator wore a plastic Santa on the maroon lapel of his uniform jacket. His mouth creaked into a smile as he bowed her into her lift and pressed the button for floor 19: Le Club Zodiaque, top of the world! The bronzed mirrors in the lift gave her a suntan as good as a Greek shipping magnate. Her shoulder had become a hump, hunched around a massive dull throb. Her white jacket gave no sign of this.

You're looking good, Frances, she told her reflection.

The lift doors opened onto the spotlit lobby like theatre curtains. The woman at the door raised weary, gold-lidded eyes and gave her an anonymous welcoming smile. A waiter smoothed his blue waistcoat and padded behind her to the round table where she always sat, next to the band and the dance floor. She guessed that her weekly visits made her a regular, for the keyboard player nodded at her and the guitarist/vocalist grinned. He was singing *I don't know why I love you, but I do*, and a holiday couple in shades of beige were making it a waltz of dance-class precision.

All the waiters were suave and deferential, but her waiter had an edge. Every line of his body spoke dignity. She ordered a bottle of white wine and a bottle of mineral water. He brought her a silver bucket of ice cubes with the glimmer of a flourish.

Le Club Zodiaque was the highest point on the island and the walls on three sides were clear glass. As usual, she strolled over to drink in the view — mistress of all she surveyed. Out at sea, the lights of a ship winked at the diamanté shore. The buildings started a whisker away from the shoreline. When you were down there, amongst flaked paint and washing that zigzagged like bunting, when you walked between palm trees and ramshackle fruit stalls, dodging ancient buses and rattle-trap motorbikes, it all seemed haphazard. From the windows of Le Club Zodiaque, the street lights made precise geometric patterns: amazingly, there had been careful town planning.

The balcony of a gold-stone house was small as a matchbox, the family leaning on it were doll's-house figures watching the world go by. Toy cars swept past, headlights small as the beam from a hand-held torch. Frances liked this place, with its sofas of opulent lilac velvet, the smoked glass table tops floating on elaborate curls of white-painted wood. She poured wine and water, and the bubbles calypsoed to the rim of her glass.

The band put an easy beat through every tune, you could waltz or smooch or shuffle. She watched a man with a shiny pink parting in his pure white hair, his trousers pressed and dustless as a mannequin. He invited his wife to dance, led her by the hand and steered her courteously around the floor, his fingers spread at her waist as if he held a work of art in his arms. They were ballroom veterans, bobbing around a tottering couple with rigid elbows who frowned at each other's feet. And frowned at each other, as ill-coordinated a double-act as Fanny and Johnny Cradock: it was hard to tell which one found the other most irritating.

Other couples took the floor. An older woman whose hair and dress were folded and starched leading a younger woman flushed with inexpert embarrassment. As they passed her table, she heard the older woman counting one-two-three, one-two-three like a jolly and exasperated gym teacher. An aunt and her niece, maybe, one paying the bills, the other offering companionship. The band switched to *You are the Sunshine of My Life* without missing a beat and only the slightest hint of up-tempo. This lured another couple to their feet: rather, a very much older man and a young woman who held him away from her, one hand pleating his sleeve. Her fingers glittered with gold and her greedy eyes raked the room over his shoulder. He was in his winter years and she was as brash as flaming June. His face said, Look what I've got, she's young and she's sexy and she's mine. Her plump red lips said: he's rich as hell and he's crazy about me, look what I'm going to get. If his heart doesn't give out, thought Frances, for Miss Greedy Eyes dropped her hands and boogied away and what could he do but follow, flinging his arms and legs up and down like a puppet.

Pain issued a jackboot ultimatum. The eleventh commandment: Thou shalt not lean on thy left elbow, or else. Or else? The penalty was another turn of the screw and worse. She shifted. Soon the wine washed through her blood, bestowing a blessed numbness. How beautifully the expert couple danced, their spines no doubt complaining with age, the woman's feet grumbling for their slippers. They'd left their aches and pains at the door and were smiling into each other's eyes.

Frances wanted to be dancing among the trippers on the light fantastic floor. Damn the dictator clawing her shoulder, she would! Over the room from her was Mrs Lily Malloy, the petite grandmother she'd partnered every week since she'd arrived. They sat at separate tables and waited until the band started its last set with a synthesised pastiche of *Hello Dolly*. Lone travellers, they'd been talking at the bar, and Lily had said how much she enjoyed dancing. No, what words had she used?

'Do you tango?'

Frances had replied, deadpan: 'I wouldn't know where to beguine.'

They'd clinked glasses and laughed and just cruised onto the dance floor as if they'd kown each other for years. The clientèle of Le Club Zodiaque was mostly ladies of a late autumn who visit a grave back home with a weekly gift of fresh flowers. Women of a certain age. It was natural to dance together. This wasn't a tea-dance with cups of tea and staid sandwiches: it was a slick nightclub where the waiters and the band flirted like gigolos. Dancing was a pleasure in itself, as holidays were, and if one has to take them alone or with friends, then why not face the music and — give it rock all! As Lily put it.

So Frances and Mrs Malloy — four grown-up children and seven grandchildren — danced together for the last couple of hours. Last week they'd shared a bottle of champagne to celebrate the birth of the seventh grandchild. She was the first girl, and Mrs Malloy was thrilled at the thought of spoiling her rotten.

'I am enlightened,' she said to Frances. 'I've bought the boys teddy-bears and Damian wanted a toy cooker and Hoover one year. And if she wants a train set then her granny will be the first to help her set it up. But I've walked past so many pretty dresses and little socks with lacy tops, I'd almost given up. And she's the youngest, so what with a doting granny and seven big boy cousins and brothers to look after her . . .!'

Lily Malloy loved dancing: she wasn't religiously correct about the steps and laughed out loud when they jived. Frances took the man's part, since someone had to and she was taller. Through the flowered silk dress, she could feel the soft warmth of her partner's body and the spring in her step. With her arm round Lily's waist and their hands clasped, she felt gallant.

But her shoulder nagged at her, shrewish pain claiming all her attention. She drained her glass, refilled it and grasped the arm of the chair. It was utterly peculiar — the wood pulsed against her left hand, strong and regular. It stopped when she lifted her palm, and came through again when she put it back. Good God, thought Frances, I can feel the heartbeat of my chair. Underneath her palms was wood, maybe the heart of a branch, or a sliver from the trunk of a pine tree. It had grown rich with sap inside the scaly trunk, buffeted by winds, rain weighting down the fronded branches. It had grown fir-cones green as apples going bronze with autumn, spitting seeds to the four winds, coming to rest in a carpet of needles. Its roots had burrowed as deep as its trunk was tall. And then it was chainsawed to a stump, split into planks, seasoned, cut again and finally curved into a chair arm. Tonight it was a living thing, vibrant in the palm of her hand.

She knew it was possible to wish the pain way, but then where would it go? Some hapless dog in the street would start to limp, a bedridden cripple might wake, racked beyond endurance, and start to whimper for morphia. She knew she couldn't do that. But maybe, just maybe, with sweet and sparkly Mrs Malloy smiling her way, she had the right to dump it. Perhaps she could let it lodge in the frame of her chair, leaving her free to dance. And as the lights came up, she'd sit down again and let the thing creep back up through her bones where it belonged. Her doctor called it rheumatoid arthritis. She was sure that at some point she'd given someone the cold shoulder and hurt them badly without noticing. It was like thinking someone was a pain. Your eyes narrow against the claws gripping you by the scruff of the neck until you let your hook of anger go. Whether planned or thoughtless, unkindness comes home to roost.

She squeezed the wood and stood up. There was a glorious sunset rush of pure-blooded warmth all over her back and right down to her fingertips. Free as a bird, she strolled over to Mrs Malloy's table.

'Would you care to waltz?' she said, with a slight bow.

'I don't know if I can-can!' said Lily, taking her hand. 'And, oh Frances, I'm being very naughty. I've ordered champagne again — for half-time. My daughter rang today and said they're calling her Lily, after me.'

'Well, let's burn our leather on the floor and then we'll drink a toast to both fair lilies,' said Frances.

They swept into bubbles of light swimming across the floor and ceiling as a mirrored globe spun overhead. Her feet found wings and suddenly she twinkled with the spirit of Fred Astaire. Her whole body was sixteen again, and the wide-eyed world was there for the taking. And since she was Fred Astaire, the dandiest of all dancers, what of Mrs Lily Malloy? Sleeves flowing gold, flame, green and indigo under the shifting rainbow of lights, she could be none other than his all-time favourite partner, the exquisite Cyd Charisse. Frances smiled at the chair where she'd left all her weary years. Oh, if it could always be like this! But she knew it couldn't and so she relaxed, exulting in the magic freedom of now.

Taking Mae West on Holiday
. . . .

S kye, travelling many miles south inside a plane, where the air is conditioned for bland comfort and the lights are recessed, neither bright nor dim. She gazed at the moonlit/sunlit clouds below her — desert, lakes, river-ribbons, an ocean. The plane came to earth and skated its mile-long catwalk. She walked across the strange tarmac. It was the middle of the night but . . .

Whooooeee! Baby, Skye told herself, it's warm outside.

Not like a blow heater that eats electricity, dries the air and rattles your mind away from any train of thought. A radiator? A log fire? All of these mean heat coming from one place and warming one place. Your feet. Maybe your ankles and legs — but not your knees. Not even a Guy-Fawkes bonfire that scorches you head to toe with a hot and lavish lick and leaves your back frosted and tingling.

So many miles south the heat wraps around you, eases into your bones; your shoulders shrug away that jacket, your toes itch to be free of socks and shoes. Skye stood by the hotel bus, basking in the unfamiliar caress. All aboard and she was nodding in the sardine swelter on seats so narrow you could lose your virtue and never miss it.

After a few days of sun-oil and cold showers, she even had the nerve to seek the shade and grumble a little at the sweat and the glare of it all. Her mind was floating over turquoise waves and she narrowed her eyes against an ocean that sparkled silver all the way to the horizon. Colours caught her eye, she caught her breath: the breakers were dazzling white, kingfisher-clear waves washing her mind clean. Flowers were crimson, flame, butterfly indigo. The light gave butterflies wings of stained glass. In an old domed church, sunlight painted rainbow jewels on the marble floor. Her bare feet drank the cool smoothness.

Ordinary people sitting, walking, talking; she printed their weathered faces on her mind. Brown eyes twinkling, blue eyes sparkling, golden skin glistening: everyone was in a movie, their clothes were remarkable, their jewellery pirate treasure. Workmen in blue denim jeans and faded navy sweatshirts had a secret life and, when they spoke, the strange words were poetry. Everybody was smoking the way they did when cigarettes were glamorous. Blue smoke, two cigarettes in an ashtray, *I love you* curling with tarry blue clouds from lips made for romance. And she was in the movie, too — a pale northern stranger, sitting outside drinking cappuccino, enigmatic in sunglasses and pastel cotton. What were her many mysteries, she tantalized herself, replaying all the loves she'd ever known. Away from it all, Skye was older and wiser: she practised a wry smile and admired her profile in the café window. She looked elegant and fascinating.

Some people were having holiday romances: they radiated an air of barefaced sin and were itching to talk about it. But Skye was too sophisticated to encourage confidences. In the evenings, she ate alone and loved it: she felt curious looks coming her way. At another table, people were speculating about her.

She decided to take a train to Arles, idly wondering whether there was any trace of Van Gogh left. She'd have been delighted with a cornfield and a few startled crows. The café in the square had a stinking hole for a toilet, the proprietor looked like Charles de Gaulle. He admired Meesis Thatcher, a woman of iron, *non*? He made bad coffee and slopped it in the saucer. He stamped and cursed at the tatterdemalion cat curling a skeletal paw across the doorstep. And paint-splattered, wild-eyed Vincent, toting his easel like a crucifix and scarlet with the sun? He'd have thrown him out as soon as look at him.

Skye ran a few schooldays French phrases through her mind. Madame Thatcher — uh — *elle n'est pas*, um, *elle n'a pas* — oh, to hell with what she wasn't or hadn't. It was time to find another café.

Vincent wouldn't just have sat in cafés all day. Evenings, yes, with a bottle of cheap wine and whatever the café had cooked that was cheap and would quench his hunger. Skye wanted to walk the streets where he had lived and see what had driven him.

It seemed that the Arlesians were torn. Their most famous inhabitant had been a crazy man, a drunk, a painter, a man who made no secret of his liaison with a whore. Their ancestors had scorned and derided Vincent and now they were rich from Van Gogh postcards and souvenirs bought by people like Skye, who only came to catch a whisper of his ghost.

That was one of the troubles of tourism: Skye needed to sit and stare to get into the soul of a place. Once she'd taken a room in a village where the bus just happened to stop. It was near a very Heidi-postcard, green and cowbells mountain, though not in Switzerland. For three months she'd done nothing there, just watched the people and walked a little. She'd be able to feel the dipping stones of the pavement for ever now, she could call it all up at will: the soft-gutted proprietor drinking red wine for breakfast, his distracted mother wandering from room to room in a filthy wrapper, his wife powdering away her bitter lines and painting her disappointed mouth pink for the soft light of evening.

City walls, narrow streets, open shutters, old women sitting outside in the early evening. Young men modelled on a youthful Marlon Brando swaggering around their motorbikes. A plant growing from the top of a dry wall. So much for Arles.

She walked back to the empty station and leaned against the wall, smoking a cigarette. A parody of a French railway official bustled in after a while: dumpy, waistcoat riding up, a gold watch and chain (station-master?), sparse hair slicked with oil. She wandered up to him.

Excusez-moi, monsieur, she said, *mais a quelle heure est-ce-que le train viendra?*

Oh, hell, he was staring at her left breast and his eyes were glittering. Jesus, thought Skye, you wear sloppy sweatshirts and track suit pants and they still think . . .

Qui est-ce, madame?

She looked down. He wasn't staring at her breast, but at her badge. One she'd made herself: a black and white Mae West wearing the smile that says *I'm gonna eatcha and you're gonna love it, big boy.*

C'est Mae West, she said.

The station-master looked puzzled, then his face lit up.

Ah, l'actrice! he said, and twinkled.

He curled one hand on his hip and patted the side of his head with the other. He wiggled a few steps and swirled around.

Celle qui disait 'Come up 'n see me sometime'? he asked.

Mais oui, said Skye.

But he was crazy about her, and how she made him laugh! My God, she curved like a river flowing, she was sexy, no? More than sexy, she was a real woman. My God, it was years since he'd thought of her, even. Mae West!

The train jogged through the darkening fields and Skye smiled at the horizon. The sun smudged long, low clouds to purple and seeped soft pink shadows over the opposite seat.

Maybe tomorrow she'd take Mae West on a trip to Avignon. See what the bridge was like, the one in the children's song where people were dancing and singing forever.

Early One Morning

. . . .

It was a Wednesday morning and she walked on the beach before dawn, early so she could dawdle all the way to the fish lines and be home in time to make breakfast and get her gran up and doing.

The breeze was chill as always, but she scented something different and faltered between steps. Her nostrils dilated. Metal? Some late night joy-riding fool of a soldier ripping up the beach with his big truck tyres? But she would have woken at the sound of an engine. Her eyes scanned the grey sand. It was smooth.

She went on.

Gradually she swung back into her easy, loose stride. Soon the sun would blaze white and clear across the grey sea and splash it into colour. Sparkling turquoise and glass-green for the shallows; royal blue and crisp white as the breakers began; smoky indigo blurring where sea meets sky. Then the dipper birds would come wheeling over the dunes, skimming the foam, light as dry leaves. She narrowed her eyes to catch the first mosquito smudge of distant cormorants — give them till daylight, she told herself. As if you can command their flight! Even the fishermen knew that cormorants must be left to do as they please: you share your catch with them and they with you. It was a terrible thing to even try and shoo them away.

'No one owns the sea or the fish of the sea,' said her gran, 'and no one owns the air or the birds of the air.'

For her the slow, wide-winged beating across the waves of morning said it was time to run to the rocks and tug in the lines and get a move on.

This morning she felt as though the cormorants were late. She shifted the sand with her toes, waiting. The sun rose smoky red behind ugly rips of dark cloud and she sighed. Storms? Gran had been muttering about storms for days and she liked her to stay close at these times. She'd been wanting to slip away today, away up the river and over the hill to a clear pool where the girls swam and giggled and the boys shifted like shadows among the trees. Sometimes, she felt she'd have to spend her whole life walking slower than she wanted to keep pace with her gran. And then she felt bad, it could be so much worse, imagine, a father and family like most of the girls her age. Houses so close you could hear everybody's business, and earth baked red and dusty to walk on! It was cool and green in her gran's house out in the trees between the village and the sea.

Maybe the cormorants were staying home today. If there was big rain they'd be wise. She loped over to the rocks and squatted, eyes still on the empty sky, fingers tugging at the lines like every day. She glanced at her fingertips as they prickled with stickiness — what had they picked up?

Her scream whirled across the waves like debris in a tornado; she pelted over the sand and through the trees like a creature when hunters close in for the kill. She dived into the house and hurled herself at her gran as she sat on the side of her bed, grumbling her feet and legs awake.

'Whatever is it?' shrieked the old lady, shaking her loose and holding her at arm's length. 'What's happened?'

'Gran,' she whispered, teeth chattering, tears gushing, a burst of high laughter ripping her mouth sideways, 'the seal All of it . . . the sea's gone black!'

Her gran's lips disappeared in a cat's cradle of lines, her etched brow crumpled a tangled web over her eyes. Her hand felt the girl's brow for fever and smoothed away cold sweat.

'Look at me,' she ordered, and her lean fingers forced her chin upwards. 'Now tell me.'

The girl shook her chin free and firmed her mouth.

'The sea is black. All of it. Everywhere. The sea's gone black.'

She slumped against the bed like a rag doll, staring ahead as if drugged.

She was paralysed, couldn't focus, knew that Gran couldn't hurry herself getting dressed and needed help. Sometimes, she almost screamed at the time it took. But now the tight spring of impatience had snapped. What did it matter if Gran took all day to bind the cloths round her aching knees so she could walk? She could take a week to grumble into the hooks and eyes of her dress. Who cares? She forced her gaze onto her hands, habit scolding her to do something. Every finger was numb and a world away.

Finally, Gran was ready.

'Ready as I can be,' she said loudly and poked her with her stick. 'This is my number one leg, girl, and you're my number two leg, so get up. Come on.'

When she walked with Gran, she could feel the trembling through every limb and felt glad to be young and strong as a tree. As they tottered through the trees this Wednesday morning, she felt herself shaking from somewhere deep inside. Deep in her belly a grey fear was crawling, blind like a worm, horned like a caterpillar.

The sun was up, the dark clouds disappeared and for a moment she breathed easy. Maybe . . .

But as they crossed the sand she could see it was true. It was high tide and the thing lay all along the sand. Gran sucked her breath in at the sight. There were no white caps, the waves were heavy and smooth and solid black right to the end of the world.

They went down to the water's edge and Gran poked with her stick, mouth twisting in on itself. The tip came out black and stayed that way. This wasn't ocean and her frilly skirts dancing up the beach: this stuff was a giant slug swelling and heaving its monstrous skirts along the sand like a curse.

It left a mark, they could see it now, gleaming on the sand as muddy swell crawled away. It shone like a snail trail but with none of that gossamer impermanence. It was heavy blackness knitting white sandgrains into slabs. Gran's stick lunged at it and dug out an ugly lump. Could it be creeping deep to infest the heart of the earth herself? Gran nudged her: something was bobbing in the black swells, shrugged further ashore with every wave. She clutched at Gran as she hooked the thing to their feet. Black and stiff like a carving made for tourists. Hideous in death, something no tourist would ever buy.

It was a bird, mummified by the black stuff that billowed where the sea should have been.

A cormorant.

She felt the thing in her guts twist and bloat with poison.

Hay, Hell and Booligal

. . . .

Alex thought of herself as mad, vulnerable, brilliant, neurotic. She had a track record of less than wonderful relationships, unpaid bills, and three hundred or so cassettes all in the wrong cases. Look, she'd woken up at two, three or four in the morning trying to plan a perfect system for keeping cassettes in order. What can you do? She had a friend who kept them caseless in huge straw baskets and crunched the loose cases to bits, muttering 'Oh, shit' as he wandered through to a five-by-eight-foot kitchen where nine wires ran from the central lightbulb. People like him made her feel positively *Ideal Home*.

She was more careful with records, having a sixties nostalgia for vinyl, although the holographic rainbows on CDs had caught her attention and she was thinking about it. She was the woman who discovered the personal stereo in the early nineties. She used it to listen to Wagner on the tube, it turned her five-foot and a small something into a snarling Valkyrie, keeping the loonies at bay.

Clothes hadn't mattered for years, of course, but towards the end of the eighties, the phrases *power-dressing* and *anti-stress eating program* had filtered through to her and now Alex dressed and ate for every occasion. When she went to the doctor for time off work, she always got a morning appointment and missed out coffee and cigarettes. She wore crumpled chinos and a paint-splashed football shirt. Doctor's surgery drag. Her head thumped, her eyes were half-closed and her voice rasped irritation. An hour and a bath later, soothed by foam, caffeine and nicotine, she could face anything, particularly the week or fortnight of freedom her performance had earned for her.

Came a point where the headaches and the rasping voice were not to be bought off for love nor money. Prolonged absences from the job meant that now she wasn't working. Her only public appearance was once a fortnight at the dole. The lady at the dole office was nicely dressed in flowered cotton, she'd seen Alex cry once and got her some tissues and everything was suddenly made easy. Rock bottom, but socially secure.

The first week she'd signed on, her lover had packed her in and moved out. It was over. They were through. Her lover said she needed time and space to rethink her parameters. Uh? thought Alex, and decided that maybe it was a maybe. She read a poem called *I am not good at love*, written by Noël Coward. Of all people! Our Noël! The ultimate smoothie, cushioned by extraordinary talent and wealth. In spite of the silk dressing-gowns, the jade cigarette holders, West End triumphs, summers in Monte Carlo and Capri: the legendary Mr Coward was not good at love.

Perhaps, thought Alex, it is a curse of genius. She even managed to giggle at herself, knotting an Oxfam scarf over her worn denim jacket, tucking a ripped shirt into ripped denims into thrice re-heeled boots. UB40 in the inner pocket, papers and baccy and lighter and keys: ready to practise her autograph!

Walking meant no bus meant she had the money for a cappuccino in the poser's café. Dole drag and arty drag were indistinguishable. The poser's café had free newspapers and she filled in the crosswords shamelessly, was even miffed if someone else had got there first, especially with a blue Biro: Alex used a black Biro for crosswords. Blue Biros just didn't look right.

The walk also meant back alleys and the occasional dustbin treasure: a jumper, a bamboo bathroom shelf, coathangers and once some perfect Laura Ashley cushions. She practised being a bag lady. Back alleys and building sites, a concrete subway dripping cold, paving stones lurching in sand and black water. Every shop at the base of Desiree House — the dole — was closed, boarded-up, wire-meshed, graffiti-ed, vandalised. This morning, there was even a fire tended by seven vagrants, roaring drunk on Emva Cream at half-past ten in the morning. Alex stomped by and declined to join them for an early-morning cocktail. She growled Nah, ta, mate.

There was a smoky curve of old graffiti across the stairs. SUPPORT THE WAR. Falklands, Gulf — who knew or cared? Someone had scratched the eyes out of an otter on the litter campaign poster. In the queue, she picked up the smell of long-term poverty. Jackets that had been second-hand a long time ago, trousers the same. The odd pair of flash trainers. Moonlighting. Years before, a Tory MP had gone on the dole and wound up in debt after seven days. He'd started with good clothes and shoes and a habitually full belly as well. After that, having proved the wrong point to his government, he'd been ignored and finally resigned. Which said something.

'Yo, Alex! How charming to bump into you! Didn't realise you were still a guest at the Hotel Desiree!'

'Dazza, my man!'

Derek was thin as a stork, his shoulders scraggy peaks under a donkey jacket. His chin was a ragged hobo grey, eyes mad with lack of sleep and *Vision*, my dear Alex, *vision*! He used to make films for BDM Productions when there was money enough for the Arts to play and flourish. Bewilderingly Deep and Meaningful — Derek was the eyes and mind of the whole project. He'd limped along under some EEC scheme which paid you to employ the unemployable until the equipment had vanished overnight and BDM became Bankrupt, Desperate and Melancholy. Derek had been terrified of being found work as a clerk or a porter, but signing on had cheered him up immensely: he too was completely unemployable. He thought of himself as insane, over-sensitive, brilliant and paranoid, and treated Alex as his soulmate.

'Would Madame honour me with her company for a small libation?' he roared on the staircase.

'Madame may be able to squeeze you in, duck, if you play your cards right.'

Derek bowed. He liked to bow and ruin the effect by keeping his hands in his pockets. They sloshed through the mudholes and stepping stones of the twilight subway, nudging each other with a staccato of Derek questions and Alex answers until city grey daylight.

'How's the old maison?'

'Yeah, Del, smashing.'

'Loft extension proceeding according to plan?'

'Too right, mate.'

'Good, good. Mum and Dad all right with the whelk stall?'

'Profits is down, my son.'

'Porsche running smoothly?'

'Dodgy, mate, bloody dodgy. All me wheels nicked.'

'Excellent, excellent. And the old love life . . .?'

'Rack and ruin, Dazza, rack and ruin. Yourself?'

'Mustn't grumble, gel, mustn't grumble.'

And Derek didn't grumble although all he wanted to talk about was his love life or lack of it. Some days it was tragedy, some days comedy. He spoke of himself as a hapless, hopeless, helpless male, seven years in thrall to an unknowing, uncaring, unattainable She. His She was married and Derek was an honourable man.

He peeled off his coat and cracked his knuckles.

'What's it to be? Tisane? What's your pleasure?'

'Elusive,' said Alex. 'Cappuccino, Daz, I can get a nice cup of tea at home. Two to a bag these days.'

'Herrings,' said Derek, hunching towards her, eyes blazing with the light of truth. 'Herrings is a rich source of protein and can be got in cans up the City Road for twenty-three pence which is less than five bob old money not bad eh?'

'If you was partial to herrings,' said Alex. 'Which I ain't. Now, your sardine, mate, your sardine is more my cuppa tea, your sardine is a fellow wot can be got for eighteen pee, about three and sixpence ha'penny, in the East Road. And furthermore, these sardines comes in a rich tomato sauce and slips down a treat on toast.'

'I had an aunt who said once, "Derek",' he quavered like Flora Robson,' "Derek, dear boy, I thrive on Things on Toast, d'you know, one can't get the help these days." I so sympathise.'

The waiter brought two cappuccinos.

'Well, how's it going?' said Alex, after a teaspoon of froth. It? Oh, love, life and all that jazz.

'I've been thinking about it,' said Derek. 'You know, if I was a boxer, they'd take away my licence. They do that if you refuse to defend yourself.'

'If love was crime,' said Alex, 'I'd ask for a thousand similar offences to be taken into consideration.'

'Any news?'

'None. I'm keeping silent. At least if I do nothing, then I've done nothing wrong. I used to think that I ought to do everything and then at least I couldn't blame myself for not having done enough. Inaction is the only power left to the weak.'

Derek sat back and smiled.

'Indeed. But I've been thinking even more about it all and do you know, I've come up with something. If BDM was still going, by Gad, we'd have a cracker on our hands. I think we could tempt Schwarzenegger with this one, what? Can I trust you?'

'Discretion is my middle name,' said Alex.

Derek rubbed his hands and looked conspiratorial.

'Well, I had an uncle who trained to be a pilot in the Canadian Air Force. Years ago. And he said that in the daytime you had landmarks to go by. But at night there were none. When you flew into a cloud you felt you were going down. Your body says, help, we're going down. Your eyes look at the instruments and the instruments tell you you're fine, you're flying level. But your body goes into panic and says — NO! WE'RE GOING DOWN! They lost most of their pilots flying solo at night. They couldn't believe their instruments and fffft! A ring of melted metal on the ground.'

He crashed his spoon into a neat circle in the sugar basin.

'I think,' he said, 'that we have learnt to distrust our emotional instruments. *She* smiles at me, and I wonder what She means. Is it pity, contempt or affection? Is she even smiling at *me*? Is it because she's thought of last year's holidays? All this before I decide whether I smile back. And then, should the smile be a light curve of the lips, a wolfish grin, a laugh, a guffaw, a leer?'

He twisted his mouth through a half-dozen versions of a smile.

'She'll 'ave you down as cracked, Daz,' said Alex. 'Now, take my bird.'

'Ah yes,' said Derek. 'The vacillating vamp, as you christened her in The Dobblers the other night.'

'Did I?' asked Alex, astonished.

'I believe you may have been under the influence.'

'In vino exaggeration. But not very much, on my money. The vacillating vamp, as I so aptly said: do I phone her? I think I'd like to know how she is. I pick up the phone. Then I think I'd like to see her, and would that be a demand? Then I think, well, if she was a friend, no. Ergo, she's not a friend, so why do I care about how she is, or want to see her. I'm furious with her, I crave her voice and touch, and I call that love. And I know she knows, but I worry that maybe I haven't said the right words the right way. By now the phone is trilling at me *Please replace the handset and try again*. I put the phone down.'

'I feel I'm being so bloody patient,' exploded Derek, grabbing the space as she took breath. 'I listen to her moaning about *him*, my friend, her husband. She says I'm like an auntie — not even a brother. I think she thinks I'm gay.'

'But what would you like to happen? Ideally?'

'Tough one, that, tough one.' Derek rubbed his chin and head until his hair stood on end. 'Ideally. Wish I'd met her ten, twenty years ago when I could still pass as a red-blooded male. Christ! I found myself looking at toupees the other day, horrible things, rat skins!'

'My son,' said Alex, 'you are on the horns of a dilemma.'

'And they are digging holes in me britches, which weren't very thick to start with,' said Derek mournfully.

It was time for more cappuccino and a cheering change of topic. But Derek was unlikely to switch tracks now. Alex had thought more than once that he would run a million miles if his She showed any interest. The courtly love bit suited his fears: if you don't ask, you don't know. Better, no one pushes you away and you don't fail. The thought made her wince with recognition.

'There is another factor,' she said, and, sensing his restlessness, she added quickly: 'To do with love.'

'Is this a drop of your actual feminine intuition?' he asked, pretending to chew gum.

'You got it, Daz. It's to do with territory. Now, we're all very familiar with the territory of trauma. It's engraved on our souls and hearts. We know just about every path, maze, labyrinth, what have you. We know every track leading to the well of loneliness, the slough of despond.'

'I'm with you,' he said, sighing. 'Why couldn't *we* fall in love, Alex? At least we can talk.'

'A little conversation before it's too late? Nah. We're romantics, old thing, we believe in True Love. And just suppose someone throws a door open in this miserable — and familiar — landscape. Throws down a lifeline, says there's another way. Suppose we get a free ride into the land of happiness? It's somewhere we have no maps for, no guides. We'd be lost. We'd soon start looking for pitfalls, swamps, dead-ends — the past brings nostalgia, and we'd get all rose-tinted and wistful about the misery we left behind us. Betcha. Think about it. Think about Shirley last year.'

'Shirley. Oh yes. She was nice, you know, she said I had a nice bum,' said Derek. 'She said receding hair was distinguished.'

'You see?' said Alex. 'You got all twitchy and bored, you probably broke her heart. I mean, she even cooked for you.'

'She did, didn't she?' he said, frowning. 'I couldn't have broken her heart. I hope I didn't. She was *nice*, but somehow it just didn't feel right . . .'

'Love is a living thing,' said Alex. 'You took one look at her love and thought, oh no, this little bud can't be love. Love has spikes and leaves that sting and flowers that spit poison. Skippety-hop, straight back to trauma land and the mangrove swamps of misery.'

'My goodness, Eccles,' said Derek, flattening his hair, 'I believe you may have hit the nail right on the knuckle. Isn't it mangrove swamps where you find blue-clawed crabs? And howler monkeys?'

'And mud-hoppers,' said Alex. 'They vanish into holes at low tide.'

It was lunchtime and, not being in the lunching class, they

went out into the street, suddenly tired and rather grey with it all.

'Call me,' said Alex.

'Call me,' said Derek and kissed her hand.

He took a long step backwards then wheeled and stretched both his arms out. He loped up the street in zigzags, swooping and making aeroplane noises. Alex laughed and laughed and the crowd in the street ignored her laughter as more-to-be-pitied, ignored Derek's flying as mad, bad and dangerously low.

She took the long way home, and walked slowly. Since it was raining and why not? What had the vacillating vamp said to her the last time they were together?

'I can't immerse myself entirely in you, I have to hold back *something*.'

The face had been kind and smiling, serious, concerned. Alex had thought, *You're throwing me away and trying to make yourself feel good about it. You don't even look like you. This feels like someone else's drama.*

She'd wanted to throw herself on the floor, kicking and screaming to make the words go away, to make the lover want to stay. But being more than ten times the age at which that sort of behaviour is considered acceptable, what had she done?

She'd said FINE.

It was a well-practised word with her. It was as tall and cold as a glacier rolling down a valley, crunching trees like matchsticks. It came to rest with corpses of slow woolly mammoths frozen deep inside, it lay on the bones of sabre-toothed tigers. It stood forever in huge, snowblasted blocks.

F I N E.

Alex brought it down like a guillotine for its utter cold meant no feeling, when feeling meant only pain. She just wanted to be on her own so that the lava of tears could flow unchecked, melt it all away.

The vamp had the gall to probe her.

'What are you feeling, Alex?'

'Nothing I choose to express,' she'd said at once, without thinking.

She chose to express nothing.

She stopped at the edge of a muddied pool lapping all the way across a back lane then leapt across to the other side. Galoshes, she thought and giggled. She hopped over the next puddle, then the next. She hopped all the way home, arms wide and waving as if she was taking her first lesson in tightrope walking. Either that, or she was a mistress of the art, pretending to trip, stumble and fall just to thrill the crowd.

It was all a question of balance.

Ilsa's War

. . . .

I'd been in the city for too long, too many late nights staring at an empty page: the Muse and I had become jaded with each other. We'd been bickering since New Year and she'd flounced out of my city flat in early May, darkly muttering, Nevermore! Three am vigils of cigarettes and coffee had failed to charm her back. So when Bernard rang and said that he and Colette would be away for a fortnight — would I like a break? — I moved in to babysit their cottage by the sea. Colette had written three pages of detailed instructions about every room and gadget. Before they left, she took me to one side.

'I have to warn you about Bernard's mother, Ilsa,' she said. 'She lives in the village, only five minutes from here. Shall we just say, she is *not* to be encouraged.'

On the first morning, I spread books on their huge kitchen table and started to cross refer. No, coffee first. Some fruit. Did my Muse like bananas? I promised myself a break with the crossword when I had written three pages. I picked up *The New Principles of Gardening*, a leather-bound tome by Batty Langley (d. 1751) and wondered when she would have been b. And exactly what had I wanted to know about mazes and knot gardens?

The phone rang. It was Ilsa.

She didn't wish to interrupt my work, she knew I was researching (that must have been Colette), but how was I settling in? If there was anything she could do, I had only to ask. I was intrigued with her voice, graciously English with a smoky Dietrich fizz. I invited her for tea. Was I sure? I lied and said that tea was a habit of mine and I enjoyed company after a hard day. I collated everything in the evening, I improvised, it would be a pleasure.

I saw her from the window, walking upright on two canes without a pause and there were twenty cliffside steps from the gate to my borrowed front door. She read the spines of my table-top library. *Memoirs of Catherine the Great. Capri. Mazes. The Last Emperor. From Peking to Paris 1912.* I played Schubert to her and she chain-smoked. Did costume interest me? Costume and manners? Then she would bring me the diaries of a grand-duchess and the poems of the Hapsburg princesses.

By Tuesday she was flirting with me in a sweet, old-fashioned way, blue eyes as young as her memory. What could I do but be gallant and adore? As soon as she sat her stiffness and the years vanished, her hands flew and the words cascaded around me.

There had been a lover somewhere in Paris, sometime in the thirties and maybe his name was Ramon. Anyway. Whoever he was, he probably had a wife in Italy, maybe Spain. Giulia.

'Yes, of that I am sure,' she said, nodding her eighty-year-old head, her ageless blue eyes sparkling. 'She used to write him letters, you see, and he never opened them. Never. He tossed them on the floor — so! I loved him. He was arr-tistic, you see. As a painter, I don't know. Probably he was very bad. But I was young and to the young poverty is adventure and romance. So — the plates in the sink, filthy with grease and turpentine, the sheets on the bed — my mother would have fainted! I opened the letters from Giulia. I suspected that he had another woman. He had. I was the other woman.'

She bit into a madeleine. With only her voice as a clue, I had spent the afternoon ransacking the village for elegant snacks and found them: madeleines, ratafias, petits fours.

'Not much call for these outside of Christmas, my love,' the grocer told me, dusting the boxes and rounding the outrageous total down to the nearest pound.

And then there was the question of tea. Earl Grey was so English, so sedate, and maybe Ilsa had been living that way for fifty years. Lapsang Souchong was opium, bohemia, late nights and Gauloises. Perhaps. Coffee? The grocer had a grinder somewhere, and his wife unearthed it, dusted it down and plugged it in for me. They had beans, they said, because they didn't get stale and there wasn't much demand. I had them blend Blue Mountain, Continental and Mocha Mysore.

'It does *smell* nice,' he admitted.

'Twelve pounds for five items,' said his wife, ringing the total. 'Champagne tastes, my dear.'

'Ah! I almost forgot. Do you . . .?'

The disapproval turned to curiosity. Astonishingly, they had champagne. One bottle of Laurent Perrier Rosé. Ordered, they said bitterly, and never collected. Jewelled with moisture, it now had pride of place in my fridge.

Ilsa accepted coffee, pleased that it was afternoon when the English don't generally drink coffee. She was delighted that the coffee was real and that I had used a glass jug on a silver stand, where a nightlight kept it steaming. It had belonged to her. Her son and daughter-in-law, she confided, drank a powder which was half chicory. Could I *imagine*? And the cups! She'd given them as a wedding present, she said, and never seen them used.

Colette had spent the last fifteen years taming Bernard. I could imagine why Ilsa was not to be encouraged.

'So, every letter from Giulia —' she went on, 'I remember that, you see, because it was spelt with a G — she was asking

Ramon to send money for herself and the children. I had decided to give up my lodgings to live with him. Well, I did a moonlight flit and stole two silver candlesticks. Perhaps they were pewter. I don't remember. I felt very wicked taking them to a pawnbroker, and then I sent the money to Giulia. I knew my heart would break if he left me and she was threatening to come and find him! But now, it is things like that which make me ask: what is morality? Shall we snaffle some of Bernard's sherry? What do you think?'

She dipped a couple of ratafias and crunched them, smiling.

'This is the way to dunk,' she pronounced. 'Better than digestive biscuits and tea. Ramon was jealous, you know? Fierce flashing eyes, and how he would pace the floor and curse. I was an artist's model, you see, and he was convinced all the men were after me. I suppose they were.'

So was I, as she drained her glass and tossed her white head like a proud young animal running free.

'People say to me, did you meet Picasso? Well, maybe I did. I wouldn't know. They were all penniless and young and burning to be noticed. One picture I remember: I was the spirit of France, holding a tattered tricolor with the Champs Elysées in flames behind me. I laughed — you know, the pole was a broom handle, and the noble folds of red, white and blue were a dishcloth. It was so cold in that studio, no wonder that painter put a torch to the Champs Elysées. He worked wearing socks over his shoes, and ragged gloves on his hands.'

She accepted an invitation to dinner that following day. Raymond, her husband, Bernard's father, would need a day's notice of her absence. She despised him for an affair that had begun and ended thirty years before. I would no doubt see him walking on the cliffs with an ancient spaniel at his heels. They didn't have visitors because it sent him into a fury. Otherwise, he seldom spoke.

'So I cook for him, it's a cross and a penance. He eats alone.

But I made him a vow,' she shrugged. 'Now I think I would have been better with a woman, as you are, no? Bernard more or less told me. Love is cruel, but I think maybe women are more gentle.'

I watched her walk back down the steps, and the wind flipped her loose cardigan so that it became a swansdown shawl. She turned at the gate and waved to me.

Someone knocked early the next morning. I was dressed to stay in and write: everything ripped and paint-stained. The theory was that the effort of changing would keep me pinned to the table, diligent and creative. I opened the door.

'Not got you up, have I? I'm Ken, I do Bernie's garden three days a week. They told me about you, but I expect they forgot t'other way round.'

Ken came in for coffee. He was a tourist peering over a painter's shoulder as he scanned my unread stack of books. Colette and Bernard self-published works about matters holistic and mystical, and Ken relaxed when I told him I was working on a thriller.

'So you won't be — wossname — testing the vibes of the cliffs, man,' he said, mock-hippy, laughing. 'I take me blasted dog along there every day that passes and all summer there's a bunch of them at dawn, wearing sheets and what not. I was born here, and if you can't see the magic of a sunrise without a pyramid on your head then I feel sorry for you.'

'Well, I think that's why they bought the house,' I said. 'Isn't there supposed to be an underwater temple in one of the caves?'

'I've never seen it,' said Ken. 'Mind, I do a bit of tourist guiding of an August and it's amazing what I can find then.'

'What do you do the rest of the year?'

'Just odd-jobbing. Gardening. I do Ilsa's garden and all. She's a lady. Took her months to call me Ken and she says Mister Reynolds when she's got company. Not like Colette! I can hear her right down the end of the garden. *Kenny!*'

He imitated Colette's intense screech. I didn't dislike Colette, neither did he, but she wasn't easy. Without her, Bernard would still be running off smudgy manifestos from a basement squat in Islington. Keeping the spirit of revolution alive until the sleepers awake. With Colette, he had graduated from a hand-turned copier to their publishing company, Mystical Medley. She dressed him in Viyella shirts and cords; when I first knew him he was haphazard Oxfam, sometimes a dinner suit, sometimes torn overalls. He had turned from a beer-bellied, ranting bear into a well-groomed, grumbling sheepdog. She worshipped him and was canny enough not to let him know. Her life was spent keeping his chaos at bay.

'Colette's all right,' said Ken. 'Only Ilsa, well, I've spent hours chatting with her. She wants her garden wild. I've put in stuff for her from all over, and she always thanks me, not like she was paying me at all. I'll bet she was a goer when she was young. Actress, wasn't she? I think she even done a few films.'

He finished his coffee.

'Well, this won't see the weeds gone. And God help those sweetpeas if they stray off of their canes. Be seeing you.'

Dinner for Ilsa. I doodled various menus. I could get fresh fish from the quay if I hurried. The rest depended on the grocer. I was used to my local corner shop that stayed open until midnight, its freezer full of dim sum, the deli counter a treasure of sauces and salads and fresh pasta. They sold exotic everything and half an hour was enough notice to put an impressive meal together.

Again, the grocer surprised me. They'd started to stock garlic and paté for the handful of summer visitors, and even had a dusty rack of herbs and spices in alphabetical order. I bought saffron. Maybe I'd hack my way through neo-bouillabaisse.

Ken was mowing the lawn that afternoon. I asked him in for

a break. I liked that about him: he never assumed the kettle was on or that I was free.

'How's the murder, then?' he said grinning.

'On ice,' I said.

'There was one I read once. The murder weapon was a frozen spike and it melted in the steam room. No weapon, no conviction. Then there was the one where it was a frozen joint of meat, and the constable sat down and had lunch with the family. Consumed the evidence. What's cooking?'

'Oh, fish stew,' I said. 'Ilsa's coming over for supper.'

'That'll do her good. He doesn't talk to her much, you know, Raymond. She told you? Sad, really.'

'I like her company.'

'Oh, there's a lot there,' said Ken, watching my face — waiting for a question? I decided to say nothing. People usually tell you more that way.

But he talked about the garden and the way Colette attacked the roses with snips. She'd bought a lawn edger sharp as a razor, sharp enough to cut your throat with. I promised to tell him all about my murder when I'd written it.

All too soon it was six o'clock, and Ilsa was due at seven. I bathed and changed and decided to start the evening with the bounce of Sidney Bechet.

I watched Ilsa climb the stairs in the golden haze of the summer evening. She wore an ivory silk blouse, frothing at neck and cuffs. She sat and crossed her legs in their tailored navy pants, shedding the callous decades with a smile.

'You can do anything, I have decided,' she said, 'if you just take your time.'

She looked at the table and nodded.

'How nice to have floating candles — see what the flames do through crystal? Have you shocked them in the village? I do all the time without meaning to. And then I think, well, it gives them something to talk about. Heavens! If I *tried* — my dear, it would be civil war. A peasants' revolt! My God! Don't tell me you found champagne in the grocery shop?'

She twinkled with pleasure as I wove a windmill-tilting, dragon-vanquishing saga of my quest for the frothy and elusive grail.

'And all because the ladies love Laurent Perrier Rosé!' she finished. '*Salut!*'

We nibbled olives and she told me about Italy. When — who knows. When she was young enough to travel alone and think nothing of it. A little after the end of the war when people were beginning to relax and reminisce about blackouts and air-raids, yesterday's terror and agony only adding a little zest to the stories.

'I was in the back of a truck,' she said, wonderingly. 'You know, the buses were a long way from normal. We'd forgotten what normal might be. Everybody piled into trucks and hung on to the doors of cars, everybody was your friend. There had been a few times, with my accent, I'd been called names, but as soon as they knew I was Jewish I had a hundred mothers and brothers and fathers to take care of me. This day, I was sitting by an old lady, almost as old as I am now, I suppose. I thought she was a hundred.

'We stopped in the mountains and everybody brought out their bread and wine and cheese, and my old lady had olives. Huge black olives, fresh from the tree. I sat with her and she tried to tell me something. *Muerta*, she kept saying. I thought she meant her sons had died in the war and I made sympathetic noises. But she didn't want that, she got quite cross and frustrated with me. Then a young man came over and spoke to her. He had a little English and he said: "She wants to tell you she is near to dying, and that she isn't afraid. She says don't be afraid of death. She says it is more bad to be frightened than to die. Death is a friend to you and you can help your friend." He shrugged and stood up, tapped his head as if she was crazy and she gripped my hand and said "*Capisce? Capisce?*" I said yes, I understood.'

I refilled her glass.

'I didn't understand, of course. She showed me a little bottle before we got back on the truck. She had it wrapped in a cloth and hidden in her dress, next to her bosom. She kissed it as if it was a relic and whispered to me *la muerta, la muerta*. I thought about her a lot and decided that the bottle contained poison and she would take it when she felt death coming. It's strange, the people one remembers.'

My amateur bouillabaisse pleased her and she recalled the docks at Marseilles.

'Where the waiters pounce on you like hawks, like desperate whores, as if you are the only girl in the world. If you dare to walk past and not go in, they dismiss you with a pout like a child, you cease to exist. On my honeymoon, we were there and we went to Les Deux Soeurs: run by two sisters? I think they were lovers. Or maybe, on a honeymoon with Raymond, I was desperate to see love everywhere. Even champagne, even the lights on the water — well, he was so English and that's what I wanted.'

She sighed.

'Everybody was charming to me, you see, I was a great beauty. In Paris I turned heads. Men followed me home, sent me flowers, serenaded under my window. Raymond — well, I don't even think he was jealous. One must be romantic to feel jealous. I think he was embarrassed. Everything he had loved about me at first became embarrassing. I used to sing in the mornings when we were first married. I would give him a fresh buttonhole every day to go to the university until he said he didn't like it. A shame. He didn't like France. Bloody abroad! Every holiday we had after the honeymoon was Scotland and rain, or Devon and tea-rooms, or the Lake District where you can have tea-rooms and rain all the same time. But by then we had Bernard and I was a mother.'

She grimaced and told me about the school playground and how her clothes were wrong. How her accent made the teachers treat her differently. That Bernard had broken noses defending her to his chauvinistic schoolmates.

'Somehow, the war was never over here. I was German and that's a crime, and to be Jewish is a terrible thing. In Europe it's different. The English don't talk about things, they make an atmosphere. It's bad manners to talk about the Holocaust.'

They had lived in London for many years and Ilsa drifted to the Polish cafés and Hungarian tea-rooms where she could talk with other émigrés and drink Viennese coffee in fluted glasses.

'They argued! They talked! They banged tables and a little old professor would shout and stab the air with his cigar. Twenty years too late and they found a thousand ways to stop the rise of Hitler, it was the only way for them to keep sane, the survivors. Guilty for being alive. Raymond hated those cafés. Like all the English, he has a pride in speaking only English and a little French. But I couldn't grow old in a city like London. I saw it happening around me. Little old women in mink shawls getting fat on pastries, resting their aching feet from tramping miles of John Lewis's carpet looking for a tablecloth. It wasn't quite me.'

I cleared the dishes and we lit cigarettes, sipping brandy. Ilsa sighed.

'When Bernard moved here, I said I had to come too, to live near my son. Raymond didn't want to. But he never wanted to do anything but sit in his study, go to the university and give the same old lectures, year after year. I said I was coming, anyway and, do you know, for one fabulous moment I thought he'd stay behind. But he didn't.'

She looked closely at me and her eyes were dark with pain

'You see, I don't hate Raymond — do you see that? Good. I

am bored with Raymond. He's everything I wanted after being a gypsy for all those years in Europe. I was everything he'd dreamed of. But a dream lasts a night and we forced ours to be a lifetime. I am as bored with him as he is with me. I laugh and he winces. He grunts and I shudder. We keep out of each other's way. And it's been better since we've been here. Yes. There are advantages. He has his dog and his walks. And I have my garden and I have Ken.'

She had caressed the name, purred over it, spoken it as if showing me a great treasure. Ken? I held her gaze and raised one eyebrow. She smiled wickedly.

'Now I am flattered,' she said, laughing. 'Oh dear, yes, I am very flattered. No, Ken is not my lover, good heavens, he'd be shocked! I can't see him as a toy boy, as the phrase goes. No. Ken is my confidant. We have secrets, he and I. Gardening secrets, you understand — what else would an old woman and a married man safe in his forties have to share?'

'Nothing would surprise me, Ilsa,' I said and she threw her head back and laughed. Was I supposed to dig for more? I poured more brandy.

She took one stick and leaned on my arm for a little walk round the house. She didn't like Colette's décor — 'everything in lines!' She shook her head at the Flower Fairy plates on the living room wall — 'reproductions!' Most of all, she disliked the lack of books.

'Colette says a lounge is not the place for books. Bernard has to keep them all in his study. That is a child who has grown up with books instead of wallpaper. Now he reads a newspaper on this tawdry three-piece suite — oh, it's not tawdry, it's — *dreck!* — second-rate. She makes him wear slippers to save her carpet. He isn't used to this, you know.'

Colette and Bernard had been married for fifteen years.

'There must be something there,' I said.

'I used to think it must be sex,' said Ilsa. 'Sex and regular meals and ironed shirts? A mother shouldn't even think about these things, I suppose. Ah, don't let me talk about Colette. I will become the dreadful mother-in-law. When he told me her name I was so pleased, but when I met her, well, she's as English as Yorkshire pudding. You know, I've tried to make Yorkshire puddings. Raymond loves them. But I can't get them right and he's so disappointed. I've had nightmares about them, even! I feel that the Angel Gabriel will ask me at the pearly gates: *Ilsa, did you ever make a good Yorkshire pudding?* Oh, it'll be purgatory for me at least, I'm sure. You know, this has been a charming evening, but I must go home. Raymond and I no longer share a bed, but he wakes at the slightest noise.'

I said I'd walk her home and she nodded. Leaning on me, she had an arm free to wave her stick at the horizon.

'Look at the moonlight on the ocean,' she said. 'There's a path tonight. If we had a sailing boat, we could go out now and bathe in moonbeams.'

I wished I had a boat as we walked down the steps, through the gate and the hundred yards or so to her door.

'Come in a moment,' she said, and we stood in the darkened hall.

'He's asleep,' she whispered. 'Come through to the garden.' But then the floor creaked and she shook her head.

'Another night, I'll show you,' she said. She sounded weary.

When I reached my gate I could still see her grey shape at the door. Whether she was looking at me or the moon — who knows?

The room we had left was startlingly bright and warm after the black and silver chill of midnight out of doors. Candlelight caught on glass, silver, copper, polished wood; every shining surface had a star. Ilsa's chair was at an angle as if she had left in a hurry. There was a little brandy in her glass and her napkin was crumpled tight. I sat with my feet up, savouring a cigarette. I could still see her eyes twinkling, hear her voice and her laughter like a gold thread sparkling through a tapestry of words. She had shrunk as we walked back to her house, her arm had grown heavier, and the air in her hall was still and old. Up here on the cliff, the night was a Peter Pan extravaganza where sea breezes dancing through the French windows turned every light to a fairy flame. Ilsa had done her Yorkshire pudding duty and our party had ended too soon.

I wanted to ring her in the morning, she'd sounded so unhappy when I left her. As I was dithering between neglected work and abandoned clearing up, she rang me. Her voice was light and easy: she had so enjoyed the evening. She would love to return the hospitality, but Raymond — did I understand? I did.

'I'm glad,' she said. 'Today is very exciting: we're going to Exeter! I forgot completely and I'm a little bit in the doghouse. It's Raymond's annual regimental luncheon — so grand, my dear! He's looking resplendent, you didn't know that he has a breastplate of medals, did you? Oh, come and have coffee with us and see him!'

Her voice blew away the cobwebs and I put on something respectable to cross the road; she sounded like a child going to a party.

Somewhere in the cut of his deep-navy suit, Raymond had lost his old man's slouch. He looked almost dapper, with a half-dozen medals balanced by a rose in one lapel and a dazzling white handkerchief in his breast pocket. He nodded in my direction and looked at his watch.

'Car's coming in half an hour,' he said. 'Good Lord, will we be ready? Hmm.'

Ilsa was in the kitchen making coffee. She wore an elegant silk dress blooming with poppies in lilac and every shade of blue. Over the top she had a jacket of the palest blue, and a brooch of seed pearls like a bunch of grapes. She looked every inch a military wife until she laughed out loud at my expression.

'It's very garden party, no?' she said. 'For this, I went shopping with Colette. Until Bernard married her, I was at a loss for this luncheon. You see, military wives don't wear pants — I didn't know. And shawls, kaftans, kimonos, I've worn them all and felt I wasn't quite the thing. Raymond said nothing. You know how a man can say nothing and you hear it all over the house for weeks? But Colette knew exactly what to buy and now Raymond will actually grunt: I've passed. Good God, it's so hideous, but it's his day. Have you told him how nice he looks?'

It would be a little like complimenting a grizzly on his fine thick fur and I wouldn't have the nerve. But for Ilsa's sake I asked him about the gleaming star and discs on their rainbowed ribbons and he became almost talkative.

'Battle of the Bulge,' he growled. 'DSO. It was awarded to a number of the chaps. And Arnhem. Disgraceful. Tragic. VC. Dashed lot of them posthumous. Terrible.'

'He was so brave!' said Ilsa.

'Mm,' said Raymond. 'Are we about ready for off?'

'Well, you both look very splendid,' I said. 'You must come and tell me all about it.'

'Waste of time,' said Raymond. 'I shan't go again, even supposing I'm here this time next year.'

'You say that every time,' said Ilsa, winking at me as she pulled on white gloves: 'I'll see you tomorrow and tell you everything!'

Although I worked all that day, by the evening I realised that all I'd produced was about fifteen pages of a rather bad Agatha Christie spoof. I'd conjured a rather camp Major Sager, complete with Jimmy Edwards moustache and a bed of roses which he pruned incessantly. He spent the rest of his time in the local bar, which I'd called The Devil and the Deep Blue Sea. He drank neat Scotch and called the barmaid a fine filly. It wasn't until he called in at the vicarage and found the vicar shot, stabbed, strangled and poisoned that I gave up completely. I felt like a jaded casting director as I banished him to the wastepaper bin. Don't call us, old chap, such a dashed shame.

I went back to Batty Langley, who considered the gardens she designed a thousand times better than Versailles. I watched *Madama Butterfly* on television and kissed the day an early goodnight with a shot of brandy. I realised I was missing Ilsa.

'I was so well-behaved, my dear,' she told me over coffee, stretching like a mischievous cat. 'My God, they should have given me an Oscar. Raymond doesn't ask much from me, and I ask nothing from him, so yesterday puts him entirely in my debt. Can you guess the principal topic of conversation?'

'I've always imagined they'd rehash the war,' I said. 'No?'

'Oh, absolutely no,' said Ilsa. 'I had thought the same thing. For the first few years, I was convinced they were being polite in front of me. But, apparently, this is the way of the English. Look.'

She drew her chair in to the table, and nodded to either side.

'Here is Major Mills. A little deaf, and scarlet-cheeked. And here is Brigadier Hillary-Jones. He has kept his figure and his bearing — although I suspect vanity might have him wearing a male corset. One could balance a crystal vase on his shoulders and know that it would never fall. He is assiduous in plying me with melba toast, and has the charm one always associates with a private homosexual. A man's man! Am I wicked?'

She laughed and sipped her coffee — *this is wine, you see?*

'In the lounge, at first, we have had sherry and they have talked about — cricket! With the first glass of wine and the mulligatawny soup — you know, bouillon with curry powder? — Major Mills is crumbling bread rolls and talking of his children: the sons at Oxford and now in the City. The daughter has finally made a good marriage, after a dodgy one. Brigadier

Hillary-Jones has nephews and nieces doing much the same. One is even in the Regiment. You know, it's like livestock, breeding, the blood lines. I talk about Bernard and tell them he is in publishing. They want to know which house he's with. Do you know, they haven't heard of Mystical Medley? Raymond is on the other side of the table, but near enough to hear me. He's dying to glare at me, but his neighbour, Mrs Mills, needs advice about a motor car. Raymond is a a man and he can't help but give it.'

She glanced over one shoulder.

'Ah, the waiters are hovering! Starched white jackets and polished pink faces, plates cleared like magic and more wine — every time you breathe, your glass is refilled. We have a sorbet to clean the palate and on to salmon mousse. Fish, you see, and so Hillary-Jones speaks of his private stretch of river. He has moved, and Major Mills is thinking of moving. He calls his wife the memsahib, so I guessed he served in India. And why, they wonder, did Raymond and I choose Porthford? Bernard again, and grandchildren. They change the subject when they find I don't have any, as if I'm suffering from a disease.'

She sighed and looked at me.

'Swathes of roast beef and perfect Yorkshire puddings. I tell Major Mills I'm an idiot in the kitchen, and Hillary-Jones spends ten minutes with details of leaving batter to stand, do I have a cold room, not a refrigerator, that's too harsh . . . I am charming and invite him to stay with us. Raymond is several shades of rose by now, Mrs Mills is a little tipsy and becoming fond of him.'

She lolled a little to one side and gave a bleary smile and a screech of laughter.

'Major Mills has the waiters refill her glass with water, but I don't think she notices. We are swamped with trifle, bombarded with toasts and the General's after-dinner speech. Major Mills has a hand on my knee, so I tell him I am furious. At this stage, anything is a compliment to him. And at last, we ladies are allowed to escape to the drawing room for coffee, and the men can drink port and talk men's talk. I gather it is supposed to be a little blue.'

She accepted more coffee, pushed her chair back and looked sombre. She lit a cigarette and looked at me.

'Would you do me a favour? I hate to ask.'

'Of course," I said.

'Would you lift my legs up? It's more comfortable. I think the correct shoes for the occasion have done bad things to my feet.'

She stretched with pleasure and wriggled her feet on the chair.

'Old age,' she said ruefully. 'You wouldn't think that a young man once wrote a poem about my ankles. God! Anyway, here's the best part. The ladies are in the drawing room, and discussing illnesses — gout and glands — when I realise there is an enormous social gaffe being performed. You saw my suit yesterday? The suitable suit? Well, it was so suitable, my dear, that the General's wife was wearing it too. This of course put me in the wrong. The foreign wife, known for her outrageous kaftans and kimonos, tries to conform and succeeds in embarrassing the General's lady. Somehow, hers is in good taste, and so mine is not. She breeds Dalmatians and opens fêtes, you know the sort? She is smaller than me, and the larger model of lady. I notice that my dress has three poppies at the waist. Hers has five. What a scandal! And I think I disgraced myself.'

'What did you do?'

Ilsa laughed until she was shaking.

'I felt something had to be said, there was an atmosphere and whispers. So I thought, now, make light of it. I told her that we should both be delighted, that there was no greater compliment than to find another lady wearing one's best outfit. She said, ah, hum, Elsie, isn't it? Simpson-Charles's wife? I said, almost, but it's Ilsa. She didn't like that much. Then I told her about my Tante Frieda in the Great War, who found herself matching the curtains at an embassy party. A story my family loved! Look, one has to laugh, no? But not the General's lady. She was most attentive, introduced me to another lady straight away, as Elsie, and said I had family in the Diplomatic Service. I guess that was Auntie Frieda and the embassy curtains. But it's not pleasant to be the subject of that veneer of English politeness which veils contempt and snobbery. It was a relief when the men joined us, wallowing into the room like walruses. They put themselves between me and the General's lady, like good house-dogs. I found their gallantry touching. But I was quite happy to leave early, which pleased Raymond. He hadn't noticed about the suitable suits, he was sure nobody had. He slept all the way home.'

'Will you go another year?'

'Oh, yes,' she said. 'Only I shall wear purple. Or scarlet. Something that will clash with the quivering jowls of the General's wife. Look, I tried to fit in and, just like always, it didn't work. When are you returning to London?'

'The day after tomorrow,' I said. Where had the time gone? Ilsa shook her head.

'I've enjoyed your company,' she said.

'I was hoping you'd come to dinner again,' I said. 'For my last night?'

'Oh, yes,' she said. 'I thought so. But I'd like to invade Colette's kitchen myself this time. I am this prisoner in my own house, you see. I have something in mind. Would you allow me?'

She wouldn't take no for an answer. When Ken called by later, he told me that he'd been commanded to show me the sights the following afternoon. We were to leave at two and return no sooner than five-thirty. He clicked his heels and saluted.

'Ilsa's orders,' he said. 'You better wear wellingtons and something that doesn't matter.'

We walked along Porthford headland with his dogs, two wolf-like blue collies with melting eyes and hearts of butter. We slid down a rough-grassed path to the beach.

'I'll show you that temple,' said Ken, grinning. 'It's a bit of a stoop for about fifty yards and then you're all right.'

He ducked into one of the caves and I followed his bent back and the torchlight in the chill and damp. Once we straightened up, he swept the inner cave rocks with the torch. It was like Cheddar Gorge before serious tourism moved in with its lazer light shows and skeleton holograms. Every surface glistened green and a sickly white. Great golden ridges hung like curtains and our beam of light was swallowed in deep gulfs of blackness. Ken played the beam near our feet on the edge of a chlorine-green pool.

'Perfect place for a murder,' he said. 'This bugger's salt, you know, goes so deep no diver's ever found the bottom. It rises with the tide, only no one's so daft as to stay and see how high. Look at those rocks on the other side.'

The ghostly beam wandered over three crude figures hunched over an altar. The rock face behind them was silvered with moisture and shimmered like a silken curtain.

'Stalagmites,' he said. 'That's the High Priestess and her two handmaidens when I'm doing the mystical tours bit. I brought Ilsa down here once the first summer she and Raymond came down. I was having kittens. But she said, take it slowly and she'd be all right. She only had one stick in them days — seven years back, I reckon. She'd never make it now.'

He wedged the torch between two rocks and rolled a cigarette. The smoke swirled like incense.

'How's the thriller going? Reckon you'll be back down here?'

'Maybe,' I said. 'I haven't got a lot done, to tell the truth.'

'My wife says there's nothing like a romance. I told her about you, and she said to get you to write a romance into your murder, then everyone'll read it. You'll corner the market. Has Ilsa told you about Berlin?'

'No,' I said. Ilsa had never mentioned Germany.

'You ask her,' he said. 'There's a story.'

Back at the house, Ilsa kissed me on both cheeks. She'd covered the table with a snow-white cloth, and she lit a seven branched olive candelabra. There was a silver goblet in the centre of the cloth.

'For you, I've created Pesach,' she said. 'It's the festive meal for Passover. Welcome to my neo-Seder table. One should do this in March, but you're leaving tomorrow so I guess September is fine. Raymond isn't fond of Jewish cooking and I may have lost the knack. It's something my grandmother and grandfather always did. My parents, too. I think I made it once for my parents-in-law. They were very polite, but also very embarrassed. The dishes for Pesach have a moral to them. Raymond's family liked to eat without talking about food, you know? Bodily functions were never to be acknowledged. I expect they made love with the lights out. It's the same thing.'

She had brought glasses and dishes from home, she said; they had been boxed for many years too long.

'We start our Pesach with matzo,' she said. 'Matzo and some wine. Your side plate holds all the lessons. That's the chicken neck that I've roasted. Elegant, no? It's to symbolise the sacrificed lamb roasted by the Jews the night before they left the bondage of Egypt. This is a roasted egg: a gift. And this is horseradish — any bitter root will do, for all the years of bile they swallowed as slaves. Salt water — well, that's tears. And maybe a hint of the miracles to come? Parsley, too, with watercress. They were looking forward to tilling their own fields in a land of plenty. Now, you don't eat these all at once. Just nibble a little as your thoughts direct you. First, we have wine and charoseth. The wine celebrates life, the charoseth is for the bricks they were forced to bake to build cities for the loathed taskmasters.'

The sweetness surprised me: charoseth is made of apples and walnuts, cinnamon and wine.

'Raymond's family couldn't quite come to terms with eating something sweet at the start of a meal,' said Ilsa, laughing. 'That's pudding, after all! I must pour wine also for Elijah.'

She filled the silver goblet.

We ate gefilte fish, and a chicken casserole, golden and bubbling. Everything was a delicious blend of tart and sweet: baby carrots with apricots, snow peas with prunes, roast potatoes sprinkled with basil.

'This was always my favourite as a child,' said Ilsa. 'Pineapple pyramids: I always felt that the Jews made them to mourn all the slaves before them that the Egyptians had broken with building their mighty pyramids.'

Finally, we relaxed over brandy.

'And Ken said to ask me about Berlin?' she sounded surprised. 'God, I didn't realise I'd even told him.'

She sat back and lit a cigarette.

'For this, I guess I need a large brandy.' She shook her head and waited until the glass was in her hand. 'Well, are you sitting comfortably? Then I'll begin. They used to say that on *Listen With Mother*, when Bernard was a child. We both listened with mother, in those days.'

She sipped her brandy for a moment, then touched her lips with a little salt water . . .

'So, Berlin. You see, I was born and raised in Heidelberg. We were a very respectable family and I was the second child. My mother made beautiful clothes for the richest people and my father baked fine breads. All very ordinary, but I was given the impression that somehow we were just that little bit better than the other families in our street. Lindenstrasse. I was made a bit of a snob. One seldom gets on well with one's family if one has the impression that one is better than them, and I used to dream that I had been found, abandoned in mysterious circumstances. I came to despise the good honest smell of bread and the deference my mother gave to her wealthy clients. She dressed me just as finely as them, and I was sent to a very expensive school. And all this meant that I couldn't wait to leave home. Do I sound very callous?'

Her eyes looked anxious, as if she wanted me to absolve her.

'I think all young people are callous,' I said. 'I was a swine to my parents for years, until I realised they were only doing their best and — the shock of it! — that they were human too!'

She smiled a little sadly.

'Now I have a child, I know,' she said softly. 'However, I leapt at the chance of studying art in Paris. I believe my mother thought of it as a finishing school. My father warned me about French men. He said to be very wary and *never* to speak with a man wearing corduroy trousers, because he would be a bohemian. Of course, Ramon wore corduroy trousers, filthy with paint. I was to write home every week. They would always be there, getting older, worrying, missing me. I said it's only three years, and off I went. You know how my life was in Paris, and I never went home. It was nearly four years later that I returned, and then not to Heidelberg.

'Give me a cigarette. No, I went to Berlin. I had been complaining that one day I must become a good daughter again and go back home for a visit. I was in love with Ramon, with life, with myself. I knew my mother would want me to stay and I put it off for months. So, when one of Ramon's friends asked me to take a package to a friend of his in Berlin, I thought, well, I can make up that I have a job and cut my visit short because of it.

'I had some problems with my papers, but Ramon's friend sorted them for me. It was like a story — my papers said Helga

Kowa from Berlin, rather than Ilsa Mancowitz from Heidelberg. At twenty, everything is an adventure. A laugh. By then Adolf Hitler was in power and we heard all sorts. You know, you are interested in politics or not, and I didn't care. I caught the train with a basket of goodies for my family, and the friend's package underneath. He'd said that if I was asked about it, I should act surprised and say it was nothing to do with me. I'd been in a couple of dreadful films by then — I think I'd swooned, screamed, kissed the hero . . . I thought I was an actress and decided to be Mata Hari for my journey.'

Ilsa tapped the ash from her cigarette and shook her head. For the first time, she looked old and very serious. She nibbled at a piece of horseradish.

'I was sitting in the carriage and a family was there. They spoke with me and we got on famously. They were Jews, I could tell, you just know. When I took my scarf off, the father looked very frightened. He told me that I should take off my David Moggan — unless I was crazy. Hitler didn't like Jews and it could make trouble for me. I laughed at him but, when he heard footsteps in the corridor, he wrenched it off my neck himself and flung it from the window. Then I began to get frightened. Wisps of rumour I'd heard in the cafés started to fall together. I suddenly wondered what was in Ramon's friend's parcel. I tell you, I was so naive.

'We had just crossed the border and the footsteps turned into German policemen. It was the first time I'd seen an SS uniform, you know. Hitler was a genius. That uniform dehumanized — the SS looked like supermen, huge, powerful, shoulders and eyes of steel. Gauntlets, as if they wore armour.

'They were very interested in me, but I was used to that from men. I was blonde and blue-eyed, the Aryan ideal. I behaved with the arrogance of a lady, and when one of them got a little — fresh? — I pretended to be insulted and amazed that he could compromise his uniform and position that way. I asked his name, very haughty. They left me and moved on to the little Jewish family. They snarled at them as if they were criminals and took their papers as if they'd like to tear them to shreds. I asked what was the problem and they told me not to bother my pretty head with scum.

'After they'd gone, the father was shaking. He said that if the SS took them away, would I go to a certain street in Berlin, to a certain family and tell them. By now the sweat was running down my back. Thinking of it, I'm sweating now. It was an hour later that they came back and by then the Jewish family had let me know exactly what was happening in Germany, and my game had become rather more serious. But I was young and thinking still of Mata Hari.

'When they returned, I became very friendly. I apologised for being curt with the lecherous one and said that maybe we'd meet for a drink. After all, I had only come back for a day or two to buy some good German clothes. I even wrote down the name of a bar and a good clean hotel that he recommended. I saluted *Heil Hitler*, you know, with a girlish giggle. The Jewish family got back their papers and told me afterwards that if I hadn't been there to see it, God knows what might have happened to them.

'How my knees held me, I don't know. I took a long way round to Ramon's friend's address and told him what had happened. He gave me schnapps and insisted that I stay at the hotel the SS man had mentioned. He said to go shopping the next day in case I was being watched. He said on no account should I go to Heidelberg, he'd somehow let my parents know that I was well.

'And he was right. The next day, the lecherous SS man met me — he said by chance. He went shopping with me, and even bought me perfume. I spent the evening in one of those awful cellar bars where all the women were blonde and laughing, and the men wore that uniform. He said to call him Hansi. I was escorted to my hotel by Hansi and he kissed my cheek. He was working until the evening of the following day, but he asked to take me out again and I said it would be delightful.

'In my room, I found new papers and a ticket back to Paris for the next day. In the morning, I dressed as if to go shopping, leaving my case and the new clothes in the wardrobe, the perfume on the dresser.'

She dabbed her lips with salt water again and crumbled some of the roasted chicken neck into her mouth. Then she sipped brandy and hunched over her glass as if it were a fire.

'I don't think anyone has ever taken a more circuitous route to the railway station. I arrived ten minutes before the train was leaving, wearing a headscarf, and attached myself to a group of schoolchildren, chatting to their teacher about how smart they were and she must be proud. I had become Greta Wolle for the return journey. It wasn't until I was sitting again in the Café des Amis, clutching Ramon's hand like a lifebelt, that I could really breathe again. His friend held my other hand and told me I'd been brave. But my grandmother had told me that if ever I was trapped, no matter what, I should do anything to stay alive. *Anything at all*. Just keep breathing and forget right and wrong, she'd said, you wait until the people holding you get lazy and then you escape.'

She looked at me, and lit another cigarette, frowning when her hand shook. Then the spark flew back into her eyes and she sat upright again.

'My dear, what else could I do but join the Resistance? Now, if I told you about those years, you'd have a story to write! I became tired with Ramon and his canvases and drinking and cursing, it all seemed so trivial. I moved in with his friend. It was platonic, for Louis was a man who lived only for the cause. I learned that my parents had got to London and prayed for the day I'd be able to see them. Although I never did. They have a grave in Golders Green: I visited it in 1947, a fortnight before my wedding. But I like to think they knew I was to be married. I'd written to them, and I feel they may have got the letter in time.'

She shrugged.

'Yes, one day we were all laughing and going to take the world by storm with our painting, our films, our crazy music. The next day, it seemed, we were suddenly grown-up and grim-faced, and the world had a terribly grey shadow over it and Paris was cold. Mad, gay Paris, where only the river is Seine, the English used to joke. Now Paris was only mad.'

She paused and closed her eyes.

'Do you know, I think I'll be disgraceful and have even more brandy. But it's your last night, and maybe it doesn't harm, once in a while.'

She ground out her half-smoked cigarette and nodded. She took the sprigs of parsley and watercress and chewed them, then lit a fresh cigarette.

'Well, then I met Raymond. Another train, I believe, maybe Belgium. Oh yes, Belgium. He came into the carriage in his khaki uniform, this great English bear with the manners of a gentleman, and asked if he could smoke. I joined him. That was the first day I realised that the war was really over. Technically, it had finished some months before, but there was a lot to do. So many people lost and displaced, so much death and heartbreak. And here was a liberator who opened doors for ladies and never attempted to force his attentions on me. So I married him. When he put the ring on my finger, I knew it was peacetime. The day we drove to his mother's great big house with its green lawns and clipped hedges, I knew that my war was over for ever and Raymond was by my side.'

She raised an eyebrow at me and gave me a wry smile.

'And now that I'm an old crock and he's an old buffer, we have our daily skirmishes — he wants the window closed, I want it open. When it's been a bad time and we sulk and grunt and ignore each other, I close my eyes and remember it all.'

She drained her glass and swept her arm upwards, palm extended as if giving me a gift.

'Yes,' she said lightly, 'you take the whole of your life into account when you are as old as I am. I remember everything. Everything. Even that it's past midnight and I must go home now, although I'm not a bit tired. Come over the road with me, it's your last night and I've decided that I must show you my garden.'

Tonight, the moon was shrouded in rags of cloud and the wind flattened the grass and swiped at the trees as we passed. Ilsa's house was dark and we padded through to the back porch like conspirators.

She took a torch from the shelf and we crept into the night, children on a midnight dare. Ilsa's garden was long and high-walled. Moonlight turned the grass to water and we walked on stepping stones to the far, shadowed wall. She stopped and drew me behind a screen of goldenrod, tangled and wild like a neglected hedgerow.

'This is a place where I only come with Ken,' she said. 'Raymond thinks it's all compost. Now look.'

She switched on the torch and the beam floated over flowerpots and a rusty, up-ended bucket. Then she held the light still and drew me down to kneel beside her. We were looking at a plant which was a little like cow parsley but smaller, its leaves more feathery. The light showed dozens of them, all the way back to the wall. Ilsa's fingertip traced the stem, smooth, ash-grey and spotted mauve as if faintly bruised. She brushed the white flowers and wiped her hand on the earth.

'I must stand up. Blood pressure,' she whispered and shone the light on my face for a second.

'No,' she said. 'You don't know, do you? That is my big

secret with Ken. *Conium maculatum?* You're not allowed to grow it, you see. But I have. We have. Ken and I. My friends. He will burn it all when the time comes.'

She laughed quietly and grasped my hand.

'My dear,' she said, 'I will never be in a hospital or an old people's home. Looking after me would be a burden to Colette. Raymond — well, *Raymond!* — and Bernard wouldn't know how. This is hemlock. Hemlock. When the time comes, I know how to use it and no questions will be asked. You understand?'

I said yes. When she asked, I promised to tell no one.

Ilsa and I wrote and spoke on the phone occasionally for a number of years. She came up to London once and we spent a wonderful evening at the opera and a morning in Liberty's. I still wear the lilac scarf she bought me. She draped it at my neck and sprayed it with her perfume: it still smells faintly of Chanel. Colette spoke of her as one of the things sent to try us, and Bernard said she was failing.

Somehow, I never found my way back to Porthford until this week, when the March winds blew me in a letter from Ilsa.

'My dear, how the days go by! Soon it will be Pesach and I think this year I will celebrate it on the correct date. Do you remember our Seder table that September? Those weeks when I kept you from your work – did you mind? It gave me so much joy . . .'

By the time I reached her signature I was half-packed and had called a taxi for Paddington station.

Very little had changed in the village street but, as I walked towards her door, I saw smoke coming from the garden. Ken must be making a bonfire.

Brightly Shone the Moon That Night

The wind woke her at six, hustling the leaves on the trees, still green in November. It gusted into every overhang of concrete, whistled down the brick funnels on the tall building where she lived. It was a busy, no nonsense and let's be having you noise. Out of her window she watched the wind whisking fallen leaves along the gutter into pavement-high stacks of yellow and brown.

The letterbox clashed and no letters came. All that hit the floor was a glossy leaflet inviting her to discover the magic of Christmas at the local hypermarket. A plastic Santa was sledging across the snow-white surface of a cake. Two candles burned. A glass of untasted wine stood at the side of the cake, a round red something at its base. What was it? A baby Edam? A pantomime bomb? She started to feel uneasy.

She could save up to eight pounds — *yes! EIGHT pounds* — *in this Yuletide Bonanza*. On the next page, another plastic Santa stood holding a walnut. He was on the edge of a table, covered with *festive fayre*: plates of beef and suntanned turkey, roast something scaled like an armadillo and studded with cloves; bowls of nuts, fruit and cream. Paper streamers like coiled fuses were scattered between the plates and wine bottles. Three dull-red baby Edam bombs sat among the gleaming cutlery.

She could garnish a turkey with chestnut stuffing balls, bacon rolls and pork cocktail sausages. *A tender turkey is traditionally the main attraction of a Christmas dinner*. Perhaps she'd find a flashing neon sign to stick in the parson's nose. Big Turk and the Cranberry Kids. The Gobbler That Ate Paris. A Sizzler for All the Family.

And why not, jabbered the leaflet, over a half-dozen slices of cheese, why not seize the chance to educate her jaded palate from the dazzling display of continental wizardry to the rear of the store?

A tureen of Technicolor sprouts looked at her smugly. Carrots curled into roses and golden hedgehog potatoes sneered: *Make this the year you take on the challenge of making your vegetables more interesting*.

Oh, yeah?

Well, why stop at a syrup glaze?

Perhaps she'd slide a copy of *Oliver Twist* into the bread bin and have a chinwag about good old Charles with her toast. The *Encyclopaedia Britannica* could be rehoused in the vegetable rack. Awesome aubergines! Did y'hear what that broccoli said about the theory of relativity? The potatoes could cast an eye over Jean-Paul Sartre and reshape their destiny: no more chips in her house, *non, non*, my dear, *pommes frites*. Should she play them music? Tchaikovsky for the onions and perhaps Stravinsky for a truly surprising vegetable stew. If she left a dictionary in the cupboard, by heaven, she'd get a good game of Scrabble out of a can of alphabet soup.

Dates should be stuffed.

She squared her jaw and nodded. The next time barmy Billy at The Queen's Arms asked her if she was keeping company, she'd tell him to stuff it. With the finest marzipan. They used to call it marchpane. Bread like what you only eat in March to keep the Lenten hunger pangs at bay.

Page three's Santa had one of the sinister red bombs over his shoulder. It was smooth and round but he carried it like a sack. Wassail, wassail, come buy our ale. Save your pennies and don't forget the Rennies. Beer and whisky make your old uncle frisky. Dry Martini, put on your bikini. A schooner of sherry will help you feel merry.

The last page was a dragon's hoard of chocolates and toffees and gateaux. Santa lugged a foil-wrapped truffle as big as himself. The baby Edam bombs were replaced by chocolate beans with ice-skates and cheeky little smiles. *Just for a treat, why not try something sweet?*

Suddenly she was ravenous, and she knew for sure that the cupboard held only labour-intensive proper food. She wanted a snack and no washing-up.

It was a strange day outside. The wind was moving everything along like a nervous policeman. A drunk and disorderly can clattered on a grating. Torn Sunday colour supplements made eyes at her from the railings. Someone had left a leather jacket on a fence and it was eleven in the morning. Why on earth had no one taken it? She wondered whose it was and what had happened to them. She feared something awful, for it hung like a rag and people walked past it without looking twice.

In the high street a golf umbrella flapped on the pavement, blown inside out, one spoke standing up like a mast. People walked round it, a pram wheel caught it and dragged it a little way. The cars were slow with the cones curving out from the pavement. A cardboard box banged her knees as she blew across the road to where an old lady was hopping on the spot and poking at a plastic bag on her foot. The wind had turned it into an octopus and the old lady muttered, 'Oh dear, oh lord, oh good heavens, what a nuisance.'

It was one of those days where she stood staring at corridors of soup cans, dithering between chicken korma and coconut or sweetcorn and satay. If you bought six cans, you got one free, but she'd only wanted tomato anyway and that wasn't part of the offer.

Then, in the queue, she was in front of Min and Joe. Min was blind and rode in a wheelchair, her head lolling to one side. Joe worshipped her and piled bunches of flowers on her lap. He bought her doughnuts and cans of Carlsberg Special, and they picnicked on the pavement and he sang to her. He sang *If You Were the Only Girl in the World* and he sang *Help Me Make It Through the Night*. Min ate her doughnuts and beat time with her can and laughed at him.

'I love her,' he told passers-by. 'She won't marry me, but I'll never stop asking. I worship her and she won't make an honest man of me. She's my girl.'

Min had a wire basket on her knees. They were buying Eccles cakes and treacle tart and currant buns and iced tarts with bright-red cherries on top. Joe had a bottle of Thunderbird too and had already opened it.

'You are my sunshine,' he sang and up-ended the bottle. Min bit into a macaroon.

She liked Min and Jo and so she walked past the newsagents smiling, without noticing until she was almost at the next newsagents, which ran out of her newspaper by ten in the morning. Only today they still had a copy. The woman was at the other end of the counter weighing bull's-eyes, and called at her just to leave the money. The sun rolled a watery silver eye behind the clouds.

In the street she caught the smell of tar. It drew her to a big yellow truck, where a dark scarf of smoke tugged across the pavement. A flame roared under a black bucket, clean blue like a blowtorch clinging to one side. Around and above the treacly bubbling, the wind shredded the flame orange and mauve and tossed the tatters like an angry juggler. Sparks flew and vanished. Five workmen stood near the heat, bare chests sweating, shoulders goose-pimpled. She could suddenly see years back, when her dad took her to smell the tar-bucket. She had a bad cold and he'd dressed her in layers of clothes so that her coat buttons bulged and her boots were tight and hot.

'Smell that and tremble, pet,' he said, holding her hand. 'Clears your lungs out.'

'Be my *love*!' bellowed Joe, behind her, steering Min round a dustbin. He parked her outside the betting shop and lit her cigarette before he went inside. Min's head was almost level with her shoulders and she smoked with a long black cigarette-holder. Her hat was a stained velvet Rembrandt, fruit lurching over one ear, and her dark glasses made her a parody of Bette Davis's cameo wicked eccentrics. She sat crumbling pastry in her pink gloves and the wind blew ash and tiny sparks from her cigarette.

Four doorways down two little girls were hollering, 'Penny for the guy.' They gawped at Min and asked each other what on earth it was. The taller one shrugged and started to push their guy away. Who's going to give money for a stuffed anorak with a football head tied to a pushchair when there's Min, life-size, with cherries on her hat, puffing clouds of fag smoke in a real wheelchair?

Joe came running through the plastic curtains waving a slip of paper and a handful of notes.

'Minnie Mouse! Ten to one!' he shouted, and waltzed his darling Min and her chair so fast that they crashed against a bollard.

'Wheeeeeeeee!' yelled Joe, jumping on to the back of the chair, and he and Min whizzed down the street, bumping on the uneven paving slabs.

'Pair of daft kids!' said the old lady who'd freed her foot of its plastic octopus by now.

'That's Min and Joe,' said her friend. 'It's lovely, the way he takes care of her. They'll be drunk as lords by teatime.'

When she got back to the flats, the leather jacket had gone.

Someone set off a rocket over the green, and red and blue sparks hung for a moment against the thunderclouds then vanished into thin air.

That night, three children knocked at her door.

'Silent night, holy night,' they sang and one of them collapsed giggling.

'All is calm, all is bright,' chanted the other two, hitting their friend.

'Round yon virgin mother and child, holy infant so tender and mild, sleep in heavenly peace, slee-eep in heavenly peace,' they finished with a high-speed wail.

She gave them a pound. It was, after all, the season of goodwill or something very close.

Oh, How I Love You

Oak trees held in perfect miniature inside an
acorn
Obsidian makes mirrors where ghosts can be clearly seen
Ocarina is a little goose and plays music like water echoes
Odalisque, peel me a grape!
O 'eck, me 'ormones
Off the planet and onto cloud ninety-nine
Oglers cast sheep's eyes
Oh, how I love you
Oil spills rainbows across a gutter
Ojai is full of domes and crystals
OK?
O, lady fair, the oleanders spice the air
O, my sainted aunt!
Onions ain't enough to make me cry
Ooh, you are awful, but I like you
Opals trap iridescence like scrunched tinfoil in amber
O queen, I am your knight and beg your favour
Orbiting the seven galaxies, my flying lady laughs
Ostrich feathers in a diamanté headdress
Otters playing, bubbles in their hair
Out of the strong came forth sweetness
Overboard and into Tallulah's lifeboat, dolling!
Owl feathers fly you invisible
Oxygen fills your lungs to float you like a lily-pad
Oysters invented pearls out of necessity
Ozone is our zest: only you know the rest

Orchids to You, Dear

· ·

S he dreamed of floating up the aisle in frothy white, to stand beside a dark-suited figure. He slipped a golden band onto her finger, but when she turned to look at him, his face was never clear. It was her favourite dream, but she knew enough to keep it to herself.

'We all have our gifts, and yours is The Brain, Hilary,' her mother had told her firmly, guiding her away from dates and dances and the like. Home and school had worn her success like a prize rosette, and she trotted off to university with a stack of leather-bound prizes and dire warnings about hard work, early nights and regular meals.

She saw him at the first lecture, and thrilled at his cultured voice. Black-jacketed on the podium, he was on a different plane from the student body, silent and scribbling at his feet. Everybody liked Professor Harrison.

'Call me Mark,' he urged her in tutorials. She had been rapt at his every phrase, pen ready to score out any word or even a comma in her essays to please him.

A matter of months later, he chose her to be his wife. He told her she was beautiful. Her mother sniffed throughout the service. Her eyes said *mutton that wants to be taken for lamb* and *my poor impressionable baby*. She took the first train home.

Hilary put it all behind her. For she loved his dapper

brilliance — my husband the professor. And now her heart anticipated his every wish, eager to change the slightest gesture, for how could he be wrong?

She had given up her hard-earned scholarship to make a home for them — she couldn't do both! He kept her in touch with the academic world, and she rushed the housework to type his lectures. He was so considerate when she lost the baby a year later, overlooking that she had failed in giving him what the nurse reluctantly told her would have been a son. The doctor said there were not likely to be others, and he assured her it didn't matter, so she must be all his family. He suggested she develop an interest of her own, generously allowing her space for something else, when all her heart and mind was his forever and ever, amen.

She opted for a sculpture class. He had guided her expertly around the monuments of Greece and Italy, the summer after the baby. But he knew nothing of the practical techniques of modelling and carving. He cleared the summerhouse so she would have a studio, and gave her the only key. How good he was!

At the class she dabbled: a dog, a horse, a ballerina. Pretty enough. But the summerhouse was for something special. She would make a bust of *him*. Perhaps it would even go to the faculty building when he retired, and they could take the world trip he dreamed of. She found the finest clay, built a web of wires to spread it on, and sat breathless at her bench.

It was the first day of spring when she began. The early light was damp and fresh as the clay when she slipped the wedding band from her finger, putting it carefully on the shelf, where it could not be lost. All day she shaped and softened the clay to build the great orb of his skull, working her fingers and palms in the heavy stickiness. Oh, she should have paid more attention to him when they lay close; she should have absorbed the hollows and smoothness of his brow and learned him by heart. Her fingertips had only fluttered around him in butterfly ecstasy. Evening found her in despair at the crude grey mass. It was a mockery.

She swathed the thing in damp cloths and plastic, and went indoors to make his supper. It was astonishing to her that he came in and told her his day, as usual, forking his food and waving the fork to show her when he had been his most witty and amusing. As if it were any day. She watched each gesture, scoring on her memory the slight frown, the pursing of his lips, and noticing with irreverent shock, for the first time, that his chin was rounded and weak. But she only loved him more.

'Are you listening to me?' he demanded when she failed to laugh at the right point.

'Every word,' she said.

'Funny little thing,' he said indulgently, rising to fill her glass. 'I never know what women really hear. Sometimes I think — everything. Sometimes you don't seem to take anything in.'

'Oh, but I do,' she said intensely, and he looked puzzled. It was not the sort of thing she usually said.

When he asked her about her day, over coffee, she was vague.

'All day in the summerhouse?' he teased her. 'Soon you won't have time for the old man.'

He felt uneasy when she smiled at this: he had expected her to defend him from his accusation of age. No matter.

'I'll be in my study,' he told her, and moments later she heard the phone click, and his low voice and laughter. How dull he must find her, to rush off and talk to someone else. She sighed and scraped a little dry clay from under her nails, letting the words of her book flow over her eyes.

When he came to bed, hours later it seemed, she was wide awake. She turned to him, and held his face on their moonlit pillow. Well, he thought, caressing her, such passion. And he was tender, and he was mighty, fuelled by an illicit afternoon with one of his students. She'd thrown herself at him, of course. And he'd had her. Right on the carpet by his desk.

His wife took him into her body, and her eyes glittered in the half-darkness. She was unmaking all her day's work, making love with him as if they'd never been together before. She ran her palms and fingertips hard over his skull with joy.

God, he felt young again! Did she suspect? Apparently not. He was confident, anyway, that his words could talk her out of any ill-feeling.

Next morning, she smiled at him over breakfast, drinking him in, for she must toil alone all day and bring him from the clay. She touched him before he left — brow, nose, cheeks, ears, chin, lips. She would not bathe away the smell of him, and slipped an overall over her bare skin.

She went to the summerhouse. Like a child who cannot bear to look at the cupboard where the witch might live, she stared past the bench and its mummified shape. She shivered, and pulled on a jumper. Her golden wedding band gleamed on the shelf.

Ready!

The head was not as bad as she had thought. But it was not good enough by half. His wise brow in life was shallower than she had moulded, and she levelled the clay with her new wisdom. The temptation to pause here and perfect his eyes! But no. She massaged the brow, standing back, closing her eyes to recall him better.

Her thumbs pressed symmetrical eye sockets, and she slung a lump of clay for his nose, patting, sheering . . . stopping herself from too much detail just yet. Time for coffee and — she hated to admit it, for he hated her doing it — a cigarette. She felt giddy with the first intake of smoke, but suddenly saw how to make a whole of the face. She smoked slowly, gulped the cooling coffee, and crossed to the bench.

The sun was high in the sky, mist burned from the chill lawn, when she stopped again. The face was there down to the mouth, and she was uneasy. No doubt that it was him. And would be more so when she could steel herself to pinch out the little chin and make it weak.

Petulant.

The word waved across her mind like a banner.

But he was not! Her mother had been petulant, shaking her head over her wasted talents. But her mother had the same sort of chin. Horrible! Nevertheless the chin would have to be done, although it loomed under his adored face like a wart, a boil. Such a teenager, she scolded herself. So he has a ... weak chin.

And it was surely only her memory of her mother that made it repulsive. She kept the cigarette between her lips as she fashioned the dreadful thing, and her eyes watered in the stream of smoke. She thought of the chin as a thing apart, and ran her thumbs down the fold of flesh to the short neck. And stood back.

She walked around it, trailing smoke in the sunbeams. It was uncannily like him. The chin was as much part of him as his keen eyes, and her face softened at the thought. Enough for the day and, good God, it would have to be fish and chips. Suddenly she was flustered — she could smell her unwashed body, she hadn't even combed her hair today. She locked the door and flew over the lawn to the house and shrilling telephone. Perhaps there would be time to cook, to bathe ...

'I've been calling all afternoon,' he told her, 'There's a faculty dinner. I won't be back until late. Where were you?'

'In the summerhouse. I'm so sorry. It's all right. I haven't done any supper, anyway.' Poor man, he must have been frantic.

He sounded mildly disapproving.

'You must take care of yourself! 'Bye now.'

Then he smiled, and dialled the student hall of residence. What a good thing, how well it worked out. He approved her new hobby.

A bath. Supper. But she wouldn't have stopped had he not been coming home. She felt daring at the thought of bread and cheese and a glass of wine alone in the dark garden. She could just see the mute grey head from the deckchair under the tree.

At her sculpture class, she was tentatively shaping a block of soapstone into something decorative, but her mind was away in the summerhouse.

'Now, has anyone been working at home?' the tutor asked at lunchtime. She looked away. He knew very well who her husband was and always deferred a little to her. None of his damn business!

Someone had been making clay ashtrays and abstract plant pots. How nice.

'I understand you have a little studio,' said the tutor.

She flushed, the little wife with the little studio.

'Oh, it's very primitive,' she apologised, and described their scullery as if it had been converted. Let him picture her pottering in the improvised chaos of a damp, windowless room . . .

But, in the summerhouse, she became dissatisfied with the slow growth of clay. He deserved the clean lines of polished marble! She would ask the tutor to get her a block — let him think what he liked. She applied herself to what she had decided was a prototype.

Which left her free to make mistakes, overdo the set of his features, and she grinned at the strange yet familiar creature, disdainful nose, full lips and ridiculous chin. Really she need only make the tongue loll a little and it could grace the pillars of any medieval church. She added fanciful satyr's curls — he enjoyed a good life, she thought fondly, and patted the damp cloth over it. In the kitchen she was cordon bleu, to make up for the neglect of the other evening.

In the middle of a frustrating bechamel sauce, the phone rang. Curse it!

'Not sculpting?' his voice was tender mockery.

'Only with flour and cream.'

'I'll be late this evening — damned tutorials. They're all panicking. Don't worry. It'll be before midnight!'

She swallowed her disappointment and told him she loved him. Then tipped the curdled sauce down the sink. She would surprise him with a picnic, and packed a wicker basket, pedalling through the streets face aglow with anticipation at his surprise. She stole up the staircase to his room, where she had not been since she was one of his students. Then she had brought her essays to be approved, now it was herself and her pannier of delicacies. The sign on his door said *Engaged*, and she smiled as she crept up to the next landing, where she knew the keyhole window that overlooked his study. How many hours had she spent here, drinking him in. She perched in the alcove and looked down.

There was his dear head, bent close to a tousled blonde mop over a pile of papers. A red-nailed hand flicked over the words as he nodded. He was so conscientious. She settled her back against the stone. And the hard chill crept through her bones as her husband's hand crept into the blonde student's blouse and they both smiled. He stood and the blonde head moved down his body, the scarlet nails deftly worked his trousers loose. She was petrified, and looked frantically at his face. Every professor was likely to be approached towards finals . . . But her husband was grinning, eyes closed as he collapsed into his chair, with the blonde mane moving between his legs. A moment later, he was lying on the student, pumping away, head buried in her neck, her pale face in a semblance of ecstasy on the rug. She wanted to go, but was frozen. They finished, and his red lips curled in satisfaction as he watched the student assemble papers and books and leave. Only then did he zip himself up and reach for the telephone. Whoever it was did not answer. Suddenly she knew he was ringing her.

I'm on my way home, darling.

He brought her a spray of orchids. She found a vase — his mother's wedding gift — and put them in his study.

At the sculpture class she expressed a wish to carve in hard stone. But not marble.

'I'm not ready for that!' she smiled.

Some grainy stone. Stone that the rain would wash over and wear way. The tutor found her an old block from a ruined church and brought it to the house. She lugged it to her studio in a wheelbarrow. She set it on the bench and raised hammer and chisel. What the hell.

And what the hell when it was suppertime. She had blinds on the window and said she wouldn't be long when he knocked at the locked door. With satisfaction she noticed how her dear little hands were becoming calloused. He told her his day. She added the blonde student, and who knows how many others. Was this jealousy? How could it be, when she didn't want him any more? Oh, there was still sex, but what astonished her in a distant way was that he didn't notice any difference.

And then he was leaving for the Devon summer school. He kissed her and pressed a list of phone numbers and dates and times into her hand. Other years, she'd gone with him. This year, he didn't seem to mind.

She fitted out the summerhouse with a sleeping bag and a change of jeans. When she went to the house to have a bath she used the back staircase, and walked through the garden afterwards with dripping hair.

She dreamed of him hurtling along in an open roadster, smiling at a blonde head and two scarlet-nailed hands spinning the wheel, reckless on the deep-banked lanes near the summer school.

And every waking hour she chipped at the ugly block, sanded, scored, chiselled, gouged gaping eye sockets. When the phone rang first, she paused, then shrugged. There was no time to lose. The finished brow and eyes leered at her and she imagined a bacchanalian wreath twined in the wisped locks of his hair.

The blonde student woke early in Devon, and shifted under the sleeping weight of his arm. How old he looked! His eyelids were pallid and wrinkled, and his red mouth was slack. His eyelids flickered and he put his sour unshaven mouth to hers. She closed her eyes and told him he was wonderful.

The clay prototype lay in shadow at boot level, dried to the colour of ash. She stared down on it from time to time. He would be back in a matter of days and there was much to do. The fleshy mouth hanging from heavy folds of stone. And the chin, his chin. She had it dribble with solid drops of wine. In the still evening, she cleansed her mouth with sips of ice-clear water in the shade of the tree where dusk-grey birds rattled to roost.

Red velvet curtains closed out the Devon night, and the bar was awash with the drunken summer school intelligentsia. He had found an ancient leather wine-pouch and was boasting that he could drain it dry. His mouth stretched as he aimed the thin jet down his throat amid clapping and stamping. *Helluva fella!* they shouted as he thumped into the chair beside the student, one hand gripping round her shoulder, the other smearing red drops from lips and chin.

In her dream, they were still careering along the road. She

floated above and ahead of them, and her eyes narrowed onto a shimmer of water at a hairpin bend. She swooped down and trailed her fingertips along the surface. Deep and cool, deep and cool. She smiled as she woke.

On the fifth day, she was almost done. Not quite. She paced around her gargoyle. The mouth. That pouting self-pleasure. She crumbled a slit between the lips, and knocked in broken teeth. Suddenly, she knew it was finished.

There he was. In stone. Frozen forever, gargoyle satyr. She was done with him.

Turning her back, she weighed the hammer and smashed it into the centre of the clay skull at her feet. She pounded the thing to grey dust and swept it through the open summerhouse doors. She cleared every surface and made coffee. But something was not complete: on her shelf, the band of gold lay in dust. She picked it up between thumb and forefinger and strolled into the garden. It made a high arc, vanishing against the sun as she flung it as far as she could.

She dreamed that night of the car they were in, the open-top funtime roadster, plunging towards that treacherous bend. The blonde hit the brakes too late and the wheels cut and thrust into the water, screaming. The car bucked and lunged against the flowered banks, shaking the two of them loose like dolls as it turned over and over. She woke with the tortured sound of ripped metal flailing against earth and stones.

The sun rose on the sixth day. She was sitting on the sill of the summerhouse and when the phone rang, she was ready to answer it.

I Believe in Angels

. . . .

Belle believed in angels. When she was a little girl her grandmother told her there were two angels beside her bed. Their wings were outspread above her like a canopy, and at the side they made a white-feathered screen for her. In the heavenly glow of their haloed faces, nothing could harm her while she slept. They helped her straighten the covers in the morning, and folded back the white sheet with celestial zest. Their wings ushered her into her clothes and flew her down the stairs for breakfast.

They steered her round puddles and away from danger. All those years before television, she glowed like the Ready Brek kid, safe with her angels all the way to school. They spoke to her all the time, nudged her to help her mother, helped her to notice things and get them done before she was asked. They suggested she sat at the front of the class, and her bright hand shot up to answer every question. In her first year she had one of those rare teachers who notices children and treats each one differently. Miss Marvel loved Belle. Such a helpful child, but never one to push herself. The angels had told her to do things discreetly, not to make a big show of generosity or kindness. Good deeds were good in themselves, and the ears and eyes and approval of the world would not make them better — quite the reverse.

Her second teacher was Miss Barnsdale, one of those who suspects a mean motive for everything. She lashed the class with scorn and ridicule and punished them for the nasty thoughts in her own mind. She patrolled the aisles like a gaoler and woe betide you if that heavy tread stopped at your desk. Little children whose faces had opened like flowers in the nurturing glow of their first year became withdrawn and cried on the way to school. They went home with pinched ears and bruised legs where she'd hit them. Parents supposed she was right; maybe children did get out of hand all of a sudden at the age of six.

Belle's angels told her that this terrifying woman suffered excruciating headaches and that she mustn't give up. They promised her that the reign of terror would be over before the year was out. She stopped putting her hand up and only answered questions when the awful voice spoke her name.

On Friday mornings after play, Belle's class did PE. This was in the school hall, and they dragged out a heavy box horse and a creaking contraption made of wood. The teacher called it a springboard. There was little spring in the ancient planks and Miss Barnsdale towered beside the box horse, ready to yank at the arms of any child who didn't manage to leap over the rough leather back first time. The fattest child in the class shrank to the back of the queue, putting off the moment of agony and ridicule. His bare feet would thud along the wooden floor and land on the springboard. He became heavy as lead and his feet stuck like glue. The teacher would haul him up and over, her angry voice taunting him, and he would try and remember that somewhere there was a mum who loved him and a dad who called him Tiger.

This Friday, the gym was freezing and all the children's legs had turned pink and orange and mauve like a winter sunset. They hopped from one foot to another to keep warm in their baggy knickers. Not Belle. She sat at the side of the room, white with fear. The teacher came in like a colossus and the class shrank into a shivering line. Maybe she wouldn't notice? But Belle heard the footsteps coming towards her and opened her eyes a crack to see the huge leather shoes next to her.

The voice cracked around her like a bullwhip. She whimpered.

'WHAT?'

'I can't do gym today, Miss Barnsdale, sorry Miss Barnsdale,' she whispered.

'And why can't you do gym today, Miss Isabella?' said the teacher, her voice sweet and dangerous as honey spiked with arsenic.

'I don't know, Miss Barnsdale,' said Belle.

'Get changed. Now. I don't have time to waste on a lazy little girl like you.'

'I can't, Miss Barnsdale,' said Belle, closing her eyes. 'My angels say I'm not to.'

'Your angels?' the teacher shouted. 'I suppose your angels know better than me?'

'Yes, Miss Barnsdale, sorry, Miss Barnsdale,' said Belle.

The class giggled, and, for this teacher, that indicated mutiny. She stalked into the teachers' room and returned with her cane.

'Well, Miss Isabella,' she said, 'let's see if your angels can stop you being punished for being a lazy, stupid little girl.'

The wood cracked against Belle's hands and she sat for the rest of the lesson holding her knees. The angels said it would be all right and for the first time, she thought, *What if it isn't?* When she went home, there was still the scarlet mark of blind rage across her palms. Her mum and dad said maybe she should have done gym, but her grandmother shook her head.

'Those are my angels looking after Belle,' she pronounced. 'If they tell the child not to do something, there's a good reason. Have you ever known her try and get out of anything she ought to do? Leave the child be.'

Nobody argued with her grandmother. Her dreams had saved lives time and again: she'd turn up at someone's door whatever the hour, her and her huge handbag packed with tinctures and lotions and bandages. Someone would be sweating steam in their sleep, someone's baby would be face-down on her pillow; Belle's grandmother knew what was wrong without being told and always righted it if it could be done.

All three made a delegation to the head teacher's office the next day. Her father in his Sunday suit, her mother in her Sunday dress and her grandmother in formidable acres of widow's black. Isabella was becoming rebellious, said the head teacher, and it took an hour to modify this to fanciful. Her grandmother sniffed and her mother promised to send in a note whenever she needed to be off PE.

In the morning, Belle had a temperature and by night, she was coughing without stopping. By the next day, there were three angels keeping vigil by her bed, one of them clad in black applying cold cloths to her brow. She got no better. Her lungs were racked with fever and the doctor took one look at her and sent her to the isolation hospital. Very few people ever left the isolation hospital and visitors had to sit behind a glass screen.

Away from her mother and father and sister and grand-mother was bad enough, but the worst thing for Belle was opening her eyes and seeing only the walls around her. She tried to pray through the fever, feeling her head trapped in a web of red-hot wires, but there was no sign of them. Somewhere between her house and the hospital, her angels had left her. She was on the critical list.

The family prayed, the class prayed, the school prayed every day in assembly. Her grandmother sat for hours looking at her shrinking face through the glass. The day came when the doctors called all the family in and gave her a life sentence. Five hours more and she'd breathe her last and never know them.

That was the day Miss Barnsdale came. Maybe she'd seen the looks of fear in her children's eyes as she talked to them, maybe she'd heard a rumour that somehow she was to blame. Maybe she was scared. Whatever. She brought a pile of cards that the children had made, using brightly-coloured paper and even the glitter tubes rationed out at Christmas.

The grandmother looked at her with Belle's unblinking eyes and she leaned forward to see the child. Dear God, she was nothing but skin and bone, and she'd been a tiny slip of a thing to start with. As the teacher looked, Belle opened her eyes and sat up with a radiant smile.

'Oh, Miss,' she said. 'You've brought my angels!'

Ten minutes later her temperature dropped, and an hour later she was ravenous. A miracle, said the doctors. Her grandmother said nothing, but nodded three times at the little girl. The great white wings wafted over her and she slept.

'After that,' said Belle, with a glimmer of a smile, 'they had to believe in my angels. In fact, they made a song about it. *I Have a Dream*. I call it, *I Believe in Angels*. Now people don't think it's fanciful.'

That Abba single was the only record she owned. She found something good in everyone. And when she came to cross the stream, she was surrounded by a host of angels. You see, she never lost sight of her dream and everyone was welcome to share it.

When I met Belle she was an old lady living in the end-of-terrace where her mother had died. All her life she fed pigeons. And dogs and cats and children and grandchildren and daughters-in-law. All living things. People who seemed to have wandered in off the street. It was as if their lives had been aimless, random as pinballs, but when they came inside her door, there was a chair especially for them and a mug chosen for their tea. She gave everyone the time and space they needed, all of creation was welcome to the oasis of her home.

I think that often people didn't realise how tired and desperate they were until they'd sat with her for a while. She wasn't a motherly type, you see, she didn't fuss around you. There were biscuits and there was bread and butter and jam and ham and you were invited to have anything you wanted. Help yourself. On my first visit, I sat and said nothing: all my conversation was stilled to triviality and I listened to Belle telling stories. On my second visit, I made tea, on the third I took the dog for a walk. The dog was an angel, she told me, and she meant it. I was honoured.

What do they say about lovely old ladies? Twinkly blue eyes, apple cheeks, a snow-white cloud of hair — forget it. Belle's hair was grey and clipped back out of the way and her skin was sallow. But her eyes were wide as the oceans, and worlds beyond human ken drifted there. Sometimes her eyes were like a satellite picture of earth, a marble swirling in space. Sometimes, they were moss green, tantalising as moss agate. Then they were ultramarine, the colour of the deepest oceans where fish fly like birds and whales bob around weightless as beachballs.

If she was reading this, her eyes would meet mine with a glint of pleasure and a steely challenge. She would be saying yes, my eyes, but what is the point? Belle, I'll get there.

You see, I didn't know her for long and it was a privilege to meet her at all. She treated herself with what seemed like utter severity. No new clothes, no holidays, no bothering doctors whatever the pain. She said that self does not exist. For all who met her, of course, the fact of Belle's self was like finding a rock in the ocean, or waking from nightmares to find yourself warm and safe.

Help yourself. Only when you can and as soon as you can. And as soon as possible, help everyone else.

You'd get no folksy wisdom from Belle, no comfortable proverbs and clichés, she spoke wisdom and truth. Common sense, she said, which is none so common these days. Yet in this austerity, there was great comfort: Belle made you aware that there need be no more lies and games. You did the job in hand the best you could and few things irritated her more than people wasting energy bemoaning the starving millions. There was plenty to do on your own doorstep — to look further was a cop-out.

If you have nothing to say, stay silent.

Everything has its price.

But this story is about angels.

Thank you, Belle, you are so very kind.

Warm

· ·

She stood by her mother at the top of a slope where the ice was worn smooth as glass by a million penguin feet skating into the sea.

'Watch me,' said her mother, 'then do exactly what I do.'

Her shiny black eyes watched closely then she flapped her wings just the same way — as if she were about to fly.

Whoosh!

The only sounds she could hear were the deep voices of Ocean. Her head burst the silver-bubble sea surface above and all at once her eyes stung with salt, her ears rang with the cold whisper of arctic winds cuffing the wavecaps.

Her mother waved her wings — come here! come back! — and called: 'Out! Out! Out you get! Dry and cold you can stay on land all day long and the whole night through, but wet and cold is danger!'

'It could be worse,' said another penguin miserably. 'It could be wet and warm.'

'Sh!' said her mother firmly. 'Wet and cold's quite enough to know in a lifetime full of fish!'

'Warm?' said the little one. 'What is warm?'

'Nothing to do with penguins,' said her mother. 'It's a silly word to have floating round the North Pole. May you never know what it means. There's fish and eggs and young ones enough to bother about.'

The penguin who had said the word *warm* shook her head sadly, and tho' the young penguin pestered her for days and days she heard no more about it. None of the colony would talk about warm and after a while she stopped asking. She took herself off for long walks to ponder in the ice and wind and snow. Cold. Chill. Freezing. Wet. But *warm? Warm?*

Then came the everlasting skies of summer where the sun hung like a silver cauldron and sent meteors of sparkle among the ice. There were even moments when the surface softened a little — just enough for her to dabble her lovely black feet.

And she watched the heavens through the months when the sun swung its wide, never-setting circle. She watched when the sun dipped away and let darkness come with its moon riding high and silver.

In the dark of the year the little penguin gazed at the wild lights of Aurora's Dancers whirling above her. Electric rainbows of mystery — scarlet, persimmon and purple; violet, peacock, saffron and jade. They danced as if hurled by some titanic juggler from below the edge of the world. The sky was filled with dazzle and the colours changed every shimmering second.

She could only look and love — she didn't have names for colours like these. She knew yellow. That was for beaks and eyelids. She knew silver. That was the gleaming scales on a fish. She knew aquamarine and every sliding shade of blue — that was the sea. But as for the rest? In desperation, she asked her mother.

Who just sighed and said that penguins had driven themselves blind, even mad, by watching that dangerous nonsense up there. She looked down at the ice as she spoke. She wouldn't raise her eyes. She warned her child against coming to a bad end. She wouldn't name the colours. Maybe because she didn't know them? The penguin was sure she did — it was just like warm all over again.

And so there was another mystery.

What did it all mean?

She grew weary of the everyday whiteness of her home and the black and white uniform of her colony. She wearied of the sameness of yellow beaks and the thin yellow line round each black eye. Her mind raced around the nameless colours in the sky and the tantalising word *warm* which they refused to speak or explain.

Only watching the sea for hours calmed her. It was never still and no two waves rose and broke the same way. The colours changed as she watched, all shades of blue and grey and white and silver. Yes, there was only the sea and the sky light carnival.

One night when the last streamers had shivered away against the dawn sky, leaving its heaven blue merely bland, she walked away from her colony and stood at the furthest tip of the ice sheet. All of a day to wait for the skyful of ecstasy . . . she sighed.

And then the sea spoke to her.

'Yo! Melancholy penguin, what's troubling your little feathered face?'

A head like none she'd ever seen before bobbed out of the waves, whiskered and grinning and as big as her whole body. It belonged to a huge and beautiful seal who said she just happened to have been drawn that way.

'I have a curiosity, small and bouncy swimmer — can you tell me where I'll find Aurora and her Amazing Acrobats? They say they dance in the sky at a carnival at the end of the world — have you seen them?'

The penguin felt dizzy. Someone she could talk to at last! Her heart raced like a riptide; her ears rang and lights fizzed at the back of her eyes as if she'd just dived deep into the bosom of Ocean. Her mind leapt as high as the moon — somehow she knew the seal could answer her heart's desire — but how could she make it happen?

Oh yes!

'Well,' she said, when she'd caught enough breath to speak, 'I am the keeper of the skylight carnival and I can let you see it. But there is a price.'

'Try me, sweet and silky diver,' said the seal. 'Only some things are beyond price.'

The penguin felt embarrassed as she gazed into the black, unblinking seal eyes. It seemed that they saw straight into her soul.

'I have a question,' she said shyly. 'And no one here will ever talk about the carnival — will you talk to me while you watch?'

'You've got it, my fine flippered fishbird — that's a gift!' sang the seal, tossing spray far and wide in her happiness. 'A two-way gift — my pleasure! I'd give anything to see Aurora and her Amazing Acrobats! But what else is trapped in your ebony and ivory throat and troubling your eyes to the brim of tears?'

'I have a question,' whispered the penguin, feeling as small as the day she'd first slid into the waves.

'Ask away, oh anxious one, for you are lovelier than an aardvark and I can deny you nothing,' said the seal, whisking the waves into a fountain with her mighty tail.

But the penguin felt too shy to say more.

'Ask me tomorrow — ask me the day after — ask me anytime,' said the seal.

That night, they sat on the ice together and gazed at the sky. And the seal waved a flipper as the lights rose like the curtains on an opera and said: 'See how Aurora casts her dice and rolls us red? Crimson and coral flames licking the darkness with warmth, glistening like blood and rubies. The hot beat springs alive and turns to copper and bronze, ringing like a sunken bell, glowing apricot and orange: all the warm fruits of the south. Oh, my perfect fishbird, see! Yellow as fine as your fish-swallowing throat, the honey-lit heart of topaz, the zest of lemon, the sting of saffron. See the way she shivers into green — how the emerald pulses through viridian veins, see the dancing jade fit for an empress to play with! And how the blue dances from sea-thistle to sapphire, she burns azure, how she winks, as if the sun herself was kissing the swirling ultramarine mouth of Ocean. Oh, the violet, leviathan heartblood, the twinkling amethyst draws us back to scarlet. Dearest wave bobber — you've shown me a living rainbow.'

Never in her life had the penguin heard so many words. If there was silence for the rest of her life she could slake her dreaming thirst with the memory of this laughing, throaty fountain. The seal had even tossed in the word warmth — she would say more about warm and warmth, the penguin was sure. And she felt safe enough to ask her.

She waited for morning, the words playing through her mind and keeping her from sleep. Finally she slept until the seal nudged her awake.

'O, she who twitches and shouts when her eyes are closed,' said the seal. 'What was the question you wanted to ask me?'

'What is warm?' said the penguin, her voice shaking: she'd asked every penguin in the colony and had her beak almost snapped off every time. But the seal just looked puzzled and kind, then smiled like the sun rising.

'Warm, little fishbird? Warm is a long way from here, warm is where I'm going — do you want to come? It's not a thing you can explain: it's like your lightshow. You've got to feel it. But are you sure? You're so used to cold that it might upset you.'

'Does it hurt?' asked the penguin.

'Warm doesn't *hurt*. Do you think I'd take you to pain? Warm might be a bit of a shock, that's all. You'll love it. But we'll have to make sure it happens slowly . . .'

At that moment the ice cracked and heaved and split around

the penguin's feet. The cracks widened and the ice shifted away into the sea.

'That's a sign!' said the seal. 'It's just made for you to travel on. An ice raft for a snowbound fishbird to find her way to warm.'

The raft sailed slowly away from the glaciers and icefields and snow and a ridiculous flapping and calling from the colony, who all of a sudden seemed to care for her and want her back.

It was far too late.

The seal wanted to race south and burn off all her blubber, but she knew the penguin was scared, so she swam in lazy circles around the ice raft, singing and talking and giving the penguin names for all the new birds they saw, birds too canny to fly as far north as the Pole for fear of freezing. They were astonished to see the penguin, and swooped low to call out with delight at her sleek feathers and solid little body. The raft she rode for them was a miracle: was it diamonds, they wondered, was it spun glass? Their feet shrank from the chill ice and they squawked with delight.

'What is it, what is it?' they called.

'It's only ice,' said the penguin. 'It's cold.'

They shivered at the word *cold* and soon the skies and seas were busy with the story of the brave little bird who rode the cold with a grinning beak and a devoted seal who would never swim far from her side.

As they went further south, the ice raft started to slip away. First, the solid crystals deep beneath the waves; the seal saw them shiver into water and become one with Ocean. She slowed their journey for a day or so and nudged some flying fish along to thrill the penguin with rainbowed crests as fine as spun sugar, spinning sea-drops in an arc over the waves.

A little further on, the edges of the raft started to shrink. The seal saw them shimmer and melt away until one day the penguin said to her:

'I used to be able to walk thirteen paces every way on the raft; and now it's only twelve.'

'That's the beginning of warm,' said the seal. 'Dip a flipper in the foam, little fishbird, and tell me what you feel.'

Oh, it was strange! A tingling that made her want to lift her feathers so the wind would touch her skin. Her feet felt weird — more than they ever had dabbling in ice-melt. Her eyes were wide with sworls of silver and blue brighter than looking at the sun at its zenith in the longest day of summer. She yanked her flipper back on the ice.

'Like it?' asked the seal, smiling.

'It's a very peculiar feeling,' said the penguin. 'What is it?'

The seal laughed lazily.

'That's your answer, my fascinating feathered one. That quavering query: what is warm?'

'You mean, *this* is warm?' whispered the penguin.

The seal gazed into her eyes and nodded slowly, without blinking.

'Come in and swim!' she said.

'Oh, I couldn't!' said the penguin. 'It's not — it's not comfortable! Sea should be cold . . .'

'As you wish,' said the seal, diving deep in a dragon's breath of bubbles.

The penguin walked to the exact centre of her shrinking ice-floe and sat with her eyes shut. She wanted to swim, but she just couldn't let herself. Not here — not now — with the sun blazing down and not a breath of wind stirring that wasn't edged with the thrill of warmth. She waited for nightfall. The sea was cooler at night, although it was still eerily different from the breath-snatching chill of the waters of her home. She swam swiftly to cool herself, but fear stopped her in mid-dive.

Only the bobbing ice raft felt safe, and every day it grew smaller as the waves grew warmer under a sun which rose a blazing orange and filled the sky with streaks of scarlet and gold.

The seal spent a long time underwater, thinking. She didn't want to trouble the penguin with the bewilderment in her eyes. She'd asked for warmth — and here it was and she didn't like it. Maybe, thought the seal, who could feel the full warm muscles of Ocean drawing her south, maybe the shock of real heat would startle her into joy. The Tropic of Capricorn was a matter of days away and the ice raft was almost gone. Without it, the penguin would tumble into the waves and feel glorious!

That's what the seal thought when she was deep beneath the waves. But the penguin's face made her uneasy. The shiny black eyes were wide with fear, and nothing she could say made any difference to the racing heartbeat.

'Tomorrow,' she said, 'nudging the last float of ice at the penguin's feet, 'tomorrow you'll feel different — trust me!'

'What's tomorrow?' squawked the penguin. 'I hate surprises.'

'Tomorrow is the end of this shilly-shallying warmth!' said the seal. 'Tomorrow we find hot, my frightened little fishbird, tomorrow the ice melts and you're free to swim with me always!'

'What's hot?' whispered the penguin.

'Hot is exactly the same as warm,' said the seal. 'Well, not exactly. Warm is good, but hot is much, much better.'

That night, the penguin waited until the seal was sleeping, singing gently through her beautiful whiskers. The seal thought warm was good? It was terrifying! And if she thought hot was better — her mind reeled. Hot would kill her. She knew it. Which way was north?

The sea slopped a careless wavelet over the last few slivers of the ice raft and one foot slipped through the paper-fine chill. She made up her mind. Weeks of floating had made her fat and idle, but she flipped into the waves and swam away in a flurry of wings and flippers, raising a snowstorm of foam.

One That Got Away

. . . .

It was a large room, with a polished wooden floor, discreetly islanded with subtly expensive rugs: a sherry-sipping living room rather than a soft-shoe shuffle dance floor. Curtains hung at the window like grey veils; the shutters were half drawn.

She sat on a chaise longue, elegant lines and the comfortless gentility of horsehair beneath an antique sateen. She felt constrained to sit and light-headed when she rose and crossed the long boards to fold back the shutters and open the windows wide. Sunlight came into the room, slanting across the boards in languid diamonds. She sat down, avoiding the huge mirror behind him, trying to avoid his gaze. He sat watching her from a deep armchair, legs crossed at the ankles, hands lightly clasped. He smiled like an engaging small boy.

But he was not a small boy. He was old as — the hills? Old as the Albert Hall.

Urbane.

She was half-turned from him, letting her eyes follow the beams and wishing she could drift through the open doors as easily as the nets lifted in the seasonless breeze. Well, it wasn't cold. Late spring? Summer? Autumn? Indian summer? That suggested a rich and golden time. There was only a slight austerity in the light: it was any season but winter. She breathed in. The air was fresh. She concentrated on the light and on breathing.

Tell me, he said, your ideal dwelling place.

She saw it at once. An old gold stone cottage nestling in a dip of greensward, stepping stones across its stream and lawn, a willow tree, ducks — white ducks and brown ducks. A sheep or three nibbling the grass close. Roses round the door. Shiny windows. But the windows were bigger than a small cottage would hold. She'd need another storey, Georgian elegance, wrought-iron balconies. Top-heavy? Friendly. She shied away from architectural accuracy — she could have a gingerbread house if it was her ideal. There was an old-fashioned herb garden at the back; the house was surrounded by lawns and gardens, shrubs and trees everywhere, beds of flowers that had been there forever. They'd come up every year, fans of ianthine delphiniums, pink tobacco trumpets dipping with the weight of a burrowing bee. Hundreds of flowers she couldn't name, she'd seen them in her grandmother's garden, in her mother's garden, in neglected gardens all over.

But what's it like inside, he said, tell me.

When it came to the front door, she found she couldn't go in. Rather, she didn't want to. Not with him watching and listening. What could she say? *The property has many interesting features and all mod cons*. The only sort of language he'd understand. Reluctantly, she drifted into this, her house, as if she was an intruder. There was a gracious drawing room, beautiful furniture, smooth with age and polish, but not the sort you couldn't put things on. For example, a chess table with elegant legs. That she played chess on. So things were both use and ornament. Comfortable chairs . . . Get real, she thought, it's your ideal, it's probably a bit scruffy, rugs and dogs here and there. People are welcome. Only those who are welcome. And certainly not him. If he called, she'd pretend to be out, she'd hide in an outhouse, hide in the straw in the barn until he gave up his snooping and went away. So now there were outhouses? It was a farm? It grew as she thought, and there were staircases everywhere, every room had two doors, and all the windows could open for her to slip through unnoticed.

They would eat in the kitchen. Which was definitely farmhouse.

This house was getting too big to manage.

She'd need a cleaner.

And her bedroom?

She sighed as she realised it was a Californian bedroom, wooden floors and a window the length of one wall over-looking trees and a river, on a hilltop. A fireplace, tapestries on the bed, a modern four-poster she'd designed herself. Silk. Cotton. Wind chimes. Music. There was music in every room. She shall have music wherever she goes.

It was hard to stay in the house. She drifted outside, restless even in the garden — was it too ordered? She climbed a tree and made a tree-house, not with planks and nails and a hammer, but with willow branches, weaving like a harvest mouse, hauling cushions and books and food and drink with her: camping outside her own house, unseen but with a view all round. She could see whoever came and most of the time just stayed quietly swaying in the beech tree. It would take a particular person to make her want to come down, into the house, and she fretted: by the time they came, would every-thing be dusty? She curled up and slept.

Tell me, he said, you're living in your ideal house, tell me now when you walk, which way do you go, what's it like, it's your favourite walk, it's ideal for you, what's it like?

Can't think, she said, can't think.

She wanted to get up and walk away, out of the French doors and over the lawn and behind the hedge, away where she could not be seen.

Don't think, he said. Feel.

What else would she be doing, huh? She was a five-sensed creature, feeling uncomfortable, feeling irritated, feeling trapped. She closed her hands and eyes and crossed her legs, breathing slow.

Trees. A river, wide and fast and shallow, pools a calm swirl between smooth rock shelves. Fallen leaves a rusty carpet except patterned with sycamore keys and brittle acorn cups. Sunlight playing like a cinema projector through the branches: it was spring going on summer. A bluebell-misted dell held the light and tossed it back to the sky. In this wood, she grew dizzy looking up at a tatter of blue heaven caught in a misted frame of high branches. There were paths in the wood: paths and no paths. Places too thickly wooded to walk, a clear path by the golden river, where flies and fallen flowers skated and dazzled in the light. In the distance she knew there was a waterfall, round a river bend she would see it and the cold and the roar would hold her silent and draw her in sure as a magnet.

Is it city, he said, is it country? Where is your ideal walk?

I do not walk in cities, she thought, she of a thousand oh God I'm late taxis, a thousand bugger the rain and the people bus stops, the never-again underground escalators and stations where acid fear turned her muscles to steel.

She saw a break in the trees, a slice of ploughed field. She garlanded every dry earth grain with flowers. Scarlet pimpernel. Cowslips. Pink primroses. Bee orchids. Wild garlic and its scent of *oh trust me, there's a change a'comin*! Cow parsley. Eggs and bacon. Eyebright. A tapestry as far as she could see.

She never picked flowers.

So that others could see them?

Because they were protected species?

Because Garbo had said I want to be alone?

Little loves, the likeness ceases!

And so back into the wood to squat and see a smudge of violets at the foot of a tree. The tree was a beech giantess and over the ladder of her roots lay the river.

Tell me, he said, okay, it's hard to think of an ideal walk, I should know! Let's say you find a drinking vessel. Tell me what it's like.

Drinking vessel. Immediately she heard liquid ringing into lead crystal. Heard a bottle gurgle, a tap splash into a cold marble sink. Thought of the endless quest for the dripless teapot. A coffee-pot glazed with pink flowers, treasure blooms. In this wood, the liquid would be cold. Cowslip wine. Elderberry champagne. Water, probably. And, although they wouldn't be high enough above the sheep line, the river water would be clean. *Eau potable*. Rain falling from clean clouds. Was it too much to hope for? But the drinking vessel . . . what would there be in a wood? A chipped china mug, utility, Darby and Joan Hall Social crockery. That strange thick white, neither glass nor china.

No.

She had once seen a glass in a museum. A glass in a wired glass case. A fine example of something or other. It was engraved as if one side was a curving window that had shattered, with a garden whiskered onto the glass through the jagged hole. Fallen shards were scratched onto the base of the stem, and a stone cross-hatched as if it had just been thrown. She liberated it and whisked it into her wood in the crook of a twisting root. That was something she'd pick up and want home with her. She dithered, afraid of picking it up only to drop it later after carrying it for miles. She took it to the water's edge and washed it, drank from it, stowed it in a root-roofed cave below the overhanging bank. She'd be back for it some time and if someone else found it? Well, as it must be, she thought, at least I saw and held it.

It's hard, he said as if encouraging a baby to post shapes through a plastic box with pre-cut holes, it's very hard, but just relax and try to see something.

A cup, she said, right? Just a cup.

What do you do with it? he said, never blinking.

Smash it, she said, just smash it.

Good, he said, good! Now carry on with your walk until you find a key. Then tell me what that's like.

She thought of the woods of fairy tale, where you find a door in a tree-trunk, a door to another land. Or where you find a tree whose top is out of sight. You climb higher and higher and higher until you step off the thinnest branches and onto a land floating perfect in the sky, with clouds as wavecaps. A land with another sky high above it. A place of dreams and danger. The sky land could float free and tilt away from the treetops and you might never get home again. A tree which led to a mysterious hole in the sky.

Wherever she went, she planned an escape route. It was automatic. The years she'd spent in London had her scanning every street and ducking into unknown buildings with their rows of nameless bells. Run a nail-file down the rusting lock and you'd be in, fasten the door behind you to delay — them? It? Whatever was chasing her had her racing up stairwells to a grey-webbed skylight, leaping across crenellated rooftops, clutching at chimney stacks, tiptoeing across high wires. Tower Bridge was where she planned her best escape: there were twin wires up along the girders, just asking you to walk up and crouch behind the dizzy blue and white towers where pennants fly. Like a medieval castle.

If he dared start to people her wood, name trees, talk of weather and subsoil and seasons, she'd whisk up the nearest tree like a squirrel, leap onto a sky island and never care if she came back down again. She could feel him somewhere at the edge of her wood. She didn't want him there at all.

She painted a mind picture of Trafalgar Square in the rain. The lions. Nelson's Column. Yes, she could see him there in the crowd, looking for her, carrying sandwiches and a spare umbrella. Good.

She stood alone in the wood. Alone was without him, and now she felt there were other people there. Woodlanders going about their business, safe to come out now that he was thoroughly drenched, pinned to the wet paving stones in a crowd in the city far away. Nagging her about a key.

Perhaps it was a big old rusty pirate treasure casket key. Or a shiny new Yale. Both useless without the lock they fitted. The new one she'd leave — she toyed with the idea of picking it up and handing it in to the police. But, just like a letter, it would sit in her pocket or on a table, a reminder of her inability to finish a task.

A letter? Write it, find an envelope, address it, post it. Sometimes letters had sat on the dash of her car until the ink was faded, like something left under the sea.

On the other hand, the old rusty key she would pick up. Parts of it would be spider-web thin under the rust. She'd always wonder where it fitted: a door in a tree trunk? Something that would open onto new worlds. Indeed, the key was such a stereotype, so perfect and impersonal, she let a smile sit on her lips.

An old key, she said. You know, really old. Ancient.

He smiled too, leant forward uninvited. Asked her: What do you do with it?

Nothing, she said, just leave it. What's the point, more clutter.

He sat back.

Carry on with your walk — until you get to some sort of water.

He knew nothing, then, of the river that flowed beside her path. Nothing of the waterfall whose roar was growing with every step. She tossed him the thought of an urban fountain; let him catch pneumonia in the November rains of the city!

Once again the woods were hers — a safe place. She was on the riverbank, lying on her belly. The moss in the river made the dappled face of a leopard, or the sleek mask of a swimming otter flattened, foaming at the muzzle. Moss sweated bubbles under the stinging sweep of water.

The best way to the waterfall was to stay close to the river's edge, swinging round sturdy tree-trunks from stone foothold to muddy slip. She crouched between root-knotted points where the river was slammed slow and lapped like low tide on the scoop of sand. On the path high above, she knew, she'd be just at the turn where the first vista of waterfall deafens and dazzles. Down here on all fours and deliberate as a turtle, she'd sneak up and surprise it.

And she did. Sat back on her heels to see and smell and hear and taste the spray of coldness misting the black pool churning at the bottom of the cliffs. The waterfall tugged her eyes upwards to its foaming crown, dragged her sight down, slipping on the sight of foam that is never still, trying to hold her eyes still. Her eyes became a film with broken sprockets in a projector someone has left running. She tried to sense the rock behind the inexorable movement and the water became a blur as she did so.

This was the bit!

She flicked her eyes to the cliffs and they rose like lands from the depth of the oceans at the beginning of time. She reeled a little at the rising cliffs where the trees flew up light as feathers. Back to gazing at the waterfall, then the tree-strewn bank opposite, and boulders shifting with elastic ease.

The waterfall was magic: she'd always wanted to fly down a waterfall, just skimming it with her fingertips, then deep into a pool so icy that breath became a thing of the past for split seconds terrifying and glorious. She could do it now, she knew — her wood, her walk — but her body became clay with a feeling of danger and a desire to survive. His eyes on her.

Let me see, she said, it's fountains, you know? I remember feeding the pigeons in Trafalgar Square, you bought bags of crumbs. Like Mary Poppins, feed the birds, tuppence a bag? Yes, fountains.

What do you do? he said.

I guess, she said, yes — I toss handfuls of crumbs here and there. Yes.

Fine, he said, fine. So carry on with the walk. You're going to come to some sort of barrier. What's it like?

Well, that was easy. Grey metal and mesh with bits of orange string, plastic orange and white bits to warn the traffic. An arrow for the subway, a sign forbidding you to cross the barriers. But she'd cross them and bugger the traffic, just as he'd expect. She wasn't there, anyway, and if he followed the picture she'd created, he'd be running across and putting his own life in six-lane danger, following someone whose coat and hair recalled hers.

And in the woods? There were barriers all the time: the waterfall itself was a barrier — a thing to be got around, no way through except magic. She hankered after a cave behind the silver falls, a cave only she could find. And maybe the behind-the-tree woodlanders who by now had noticed her, she felt sure. Barriers? Fallen trees a summer palace for woodlice and earwigs, a palace rococo with fungi and avenues of emerald moss. A young tree she could leap over without damage, an older tree she'd go around, look at the storm-gouged roots clumped with stones, even the hopeful start of a sapling in the dead wood. The new hollow below was already green with nettles and wild mint.

She supposed that somewhere there might be a fence, some fool imagining that evenly-spaced and wired poles made the land his. But maybe not. Maybe in the world of this wood those days were gone and all she'd find at the edge of the trees would be dry-stone walls, left to crumble. Where sheep may safely graze.

She could even hear them bleating. Somewhere outside,

among the dusty sunbeams . . .

She was at the open French door and the lawns spread before her to an old wrought-iron fence. Beyond, there was a late afternoon flock of sheep, etched in sunlight. She looked back at the shaded room. It was like a neglected fish tank, her face was a splash of white in the mirror.

She was aware that he was still sitting there. That he might always be sitting there, waiting to hear someone else's dream. Waiting for the dream that would take him in.

She ran across the lawn towards the bright green meadow.

Stars

· ·

My grandparents lived in a small town by the sea. Over the hill from their bungalow was the Bristol Channel. My grandma loved her garden and she grew roses and lavender and marigolds. In the back garden, there was an old and dusty summerhouse, the sort that turned like a sunflower to face the sun. Though not when I knew it: when I was a child, spiders with legs like umbrella spokes lived there and the floor was sad with curled-up leaves and dust.

One year, we were there for Hallowe'en and my sister and I hollowed out pumpkins with triangle eyes and jagged teeth. We lit candles inside them and scared ourselves silly putting them on the church wall over the road. Behind the wall was a graveyard, all in shadow. Damp, dank, black and green stones carved deep for the sorely missed, the dear departed, the sleeping. We raced back through the frosty dark and crouched behind grandma's garden wall to see if any cars crashed in terror. They didn't, although one swerved a bit.

My grandma gave us presents when we came to stay. One year, she gave me a ball. I could tell from the paper-wrapped shape and I wasn't that thrilled. I pretended, because I loved my grandma. But when I took the paper off, it was magic. A starry ball. It was red and the five-pointed stars were yellow and it was the most beautiful ball in the whole world and I loved it.

I bounced it in the garden, I kicked it on the lawn, I put it on the cabinet next to my bed. My grandma's mattresses were feather and you rolled into the dip in the middle and stayed there all night. Morning was like climbing out of a nest.

There was a clock in the hall that rang the quarter-hours. Westminster chimes, my mother said. The words were as comforting and gracious as the sound of the clock. I'll know I've settled down when I get a clock like that, ringing soft like old bells inside waxed caramel whorls of wood, numbers and hands curling like old-fashioned handwriting: the sort that says Dear Sir, With reference to yrs. of the 5th inst. A more restrained version of the signature of Elizabeth I, riding on curlicued wavecaps of ink.

They had a framed picture of *The Street Cries of Old London*: little girls with rosy cheeks in big boots and tattered shawls carrying wicker baskets piled with violets, cherries and sweet lavender. In the kitchen, my aunt made a weekly batch of biscuits with butter and flour and vanilla essence, dusted with sugar and stored in tall glass jars with frosted stoppers.

My grandpa creaked when he walked. The folding door to the sitting room creaked open and shut. Grandpa would sit smoking with an ashtray as big as a dog's bowl at his feet. The ash grew on his cigarette and never dropped. He would take the stub and its frozen ash from his lips and place it in the bowl unbroken. He sat for hours and I sat watching him, a book on my knee.

The photos on the mantelpiece were faded blue in silver frames: my parents' wedding, my grandparents' golden wedding, my sister and I in the cardigans grandma knitted for us. My auntie's dog.

We would go out for rides in the car, an Austin A40, which meant tartan rugs and being squashed in the back with Grandpa and a black velvet cushion. Grandpa told us about crystal wireless sets and the first aeroplane and when they ran through the streets of Bristol cheering because a car had been made that would go at sixty miles an hour. A mile a minute! We'd stop for ice cream and my sister and I were let out to run on the grass or the beach, like puppies.

Most of the time we went for walks. There was the walk turning left at the garden gate, up the lane and over the hill. There was the walk turning right, up the lane past a house where a man kept a monkey for a pet, my aunt told us. The front door was ivied over, and the side porch door had frosted glass. Often I'd creep up to the gate and see if I could see the shape of the monkey swinging wildly all over the place. I had a good deal of respect for monkeys and apes. Anthropoids, I'd say to myself. I'd just read *Tarzan of the Apes* by Edgar Rice Burroughs and it was the greatest book in the world.

'Her hair was turned to burnished gold in the dying rays of the setting sun.'

That's what it said in Tarzan, and I knew it was the most marvellous sentence I'd ever read. It was exotic, like the square cakes in my tin paintbox. Vermilion, Carmine, Burnt Umber, Emerald, Burnt Sienna, Crimson Lake.

Nothing ever moved inside the monkey's house, even if I went past then turned quick as a flash to catch them out. After that, the walk went up the lane by the church and over a dip in the stone wall where once there had been a stile. The path became steep and winding, round stones worn smooth and fringed with grass. I threw my starry ball and it ran back toward me or stopped in a dip until I picked it up again.

One day, I threw it — higher? sideways? — further than before. The path curved here and I couldn't see the starry ball. It hadn't gone rolling down the path past me. Oh well, it must be in the bushes. My mother always put me in trousers outside schooltime, unless we were visiting or going to church. There was a massive tangle of brambles sprouting from dead tree stumps like Medusa's awful hair. I waded in, wishing I had wellingtons, kicking nettles flat out of my way, spiked magenta blackberry stems catching my sleeves. I couldn't see anything round or red or yellow, but I went deeper and deeper, right under the damp rotting wood, cringing at woodlice — grannies — centipedes, rivulets of white flaky fungi. If the ground hadn't been black and soggy with leaves and a fleshy, naked slug, I'd have sat down and howled.

It couldn't have gone far. I shoved my toes into the stones of the wall and hung over the edge of a field. The ground swept downwards and up again and there was nothing but sheep and grass cropped short by sheep. It was harder to get up on the bramble-side wall, the stones were higgledy-piggledy with moss and rusting wire. Over the top, I dropped onto layers of damp leaves. I combed the copse, weak with fear when I stumbled on a circle of charred grass and bottles with crisp packets wet with dew. People had been here and might still be hiding behind trees, watching and waiting. I started to sing, loud and brave.

Maybe I'd missed something under the spiked serpent lair. This time the thorns tore my hair and hands and I sucked the scratches, beaded with blood: did that make me a cannibal? I made myself crouch and peer, despite the slug and the gunmetal grannies and dangerous fire-red spiders swarming on the torn branches.

I knew they wouldn't be that cross. They never were when we stayed at Grandma's. That afternoon I got my dad to come with me. He strode through brambles and nettles and never noticed them. But even he couldn't find my starry ball. We picked up the crisp packets and bottles and he said maybe someone else had found it while we were having lunch. I couldn't see that: I'd never met anyone on this path, I felt it was ours. No, it was mine. So some thieving cheat of a boy had pinched my best toy ever? We went to the seaside the next day and I scoured the beach, glaring at every child, seeing my starry ball everywhere.

And nowhere.

All that week I searched, though I knew it was useless. And I knew what happened to things left out in the rain. I could picture the scarlet shine fading to a dull pink, the bright yellow stars going pale as cream, the taut roundness sagging in on itself like a dying balloon.

In bed on the last night I prayed God bless Mummy, Daddy, Grandma, Grandpa, Auntie, my sister and everyone else that I can't remember — my cover-all addition. I'd heard them talking earlier on, and someone said that children have to learn, you know. All the same, I crossed my fingers and hoped that Grandma would give me another starry ball.

The next time we went to see them, she gave me a torch. I wasn't that thrilled. But my dad took me walking up the hill in the dark and showed me how to make amazing shadows with every tree and gravestone. We stopped on the headland and I shone the beam straight up into the night, all the way to the stars.

Time After Time

∙ ∙

'It's nice of you to visit,' she said. 'I've been lying here thinking and there's so much I want you to know.'

'Tell me,' I said. 'Tell me everything.'

'I'll tell you all there's time for,' she said. 'Could you do something with these pillows? I don't know what, but they seem so hard. Or maybe my bones have gone soft. It happens, you know.'

I slid one arm round her back and lifted her forward. My other arm worked some air through the cotton and feathers and when I let her lie back again, she smiled. Her hand came up to brush my face. Her skin was silver and brown with age and felt like satin.

'You see,' she said, 'you've done it. Let me think.'

Her eyelids went down over her weary, clouded eyes and the nerves in her face fluttered for a while. Then she looked straight at me and her gaze was clear as daylight.

'Let me see,' she said. 'Where did I begin? Oh yes. I was a woman serving in a Roman house where the master was a writer, a philosopher possibly, whatever: he employed a dozen scribes to record his words. It was my job to carry water, to cook, to clean, to look after the master's children, to bathe and dress the mistress.

'I was a slave, I suppose, although when you know nothing different, the word doesn't fill you with those high emotions I'd feel now. To be a slave: I'd rage, despair, rebel! But I remember feeling only awe and longing when I passed the high cool room where the scribes worked. Sitting quietly all day and writing, leaving their work to come to meals already prepared, leaving the table and its dirty dishes to return to their mysterious work. Was it envy? I wanted to join them, to work as they did, I didn't want to take it from them. I learned to serve.

'Then there was a time when I was married, I believe. There were children and I loved them. Again, the work of a house and family was my lot, only this time it was my house, my family, my blood. It's different from taking orders, making your own order. Perhaps I didn't understand children — who ever understands anyone else? But perhaps I didn't understand them well enough.

'You see, after that I was a boy without parents, longing to belong. I was a poor boy who was sent to sea and, ever since, my blood has thrilled to the creak of ropes and the proud lines of old ships. I was a cabin boy, a dogsbody, the one they sent up the rigging to see where we were going, the one who hung over the side gawping at the clear waters and strange fish who swam below, gawping up at me. There was a storm, I drowned.

'Since then, I have always been able to swim like a fish and there is always youth in my heart. When people have done their best to pour cold water on my enthusiasms, and tried to undermine me as immature, somewhere my thirteen-year-old boy rubs his bare toe on a scrubbed deck and flushes with rebellion, tosses his head back with defiance and says, yah, I don't care. They've done their best to stop me doing my best, but it's never worked for long.

'And there was a long, dark life when I was a prostitute and, my God, another darker time I was a prostitute again. The first was so bad that I killed myself and had to come back and learn it all again. My body is my own now. However bad it's been, I've never committed suicide since, although — this time, when you and I have met, once, in the darkest months, I gathered the instruments of my own death and kept them to hand. Just in case, but hoping against it, because this time I seem to know so much of what I need to learn. This time I've been lucky.

'I have killed and been killed. Even now, I wake up with nightmares about killing.

'So I know the worst.

'They are suicide, cruelty, murder, meanness, lying.

'The best is like dreams you hate to wake from. To love and be loved all at the same time. Friends. Happiness. Stories. Trees and flowers.

'Trees always. As a small boy on the ship, I knew the mast was a tree and I was safe there. This time, visiting the house of a great man of letters, his staircase had as its heart the trunk of an oak. I walked up with my hand on the smoothed trunk. No words. See the tree outside my window? I knew.

'I've never been wealthy, because I still wonder what it would be like. I think I have the wisdom to see that it's not a goal. I don't want it. Enough contributes to happiness, excess is a ball and chain, a fiscal vampire. Look at the wealthy of the world — it's not a good advertisement. Wealth brings you power in other people's lives: it's a grave responsibility!'

She sat upright now and held my hand, staring towards the window, nodding as the branches of a tree might nod in a light breeze.

'My dear,' she said, 'so much to tell you. So short a time.

'What drew us here first, do you think, what was so strong that it pulled us into this world of clay and decay?

'It was the adventures and pleasures of the senses.

'Sight and the vari-coloured eyes that own it. The myriad

forms and colours of this planet. We influence and inform it, of course, with that immortal, joyous why-not that makes a million different trees and leaves and flowers and fruits, where the function is simply to produce oxygen and cleanse the air for the continuation of life. But clay fights its own needs and chops down trees for chipboard to hold setting concrete on skyscrapers where the air is conditioned. They call it progress. I hope it's circular progress, a true revolution where you return to your starting point with wisdom and knowledge. Ah, sight! Another person walks into a room and our being lights up.

'The five senses seduced us into life. Do you see?'

I clasped her fingers, alive with an urgent pulse.

'The five senses,' she whispered, 'My God, how lovely! Think of it! Smell: the tang of woodsmoke, the fragrance of a field or a wood and its changing scents in the rain and the sun. The refinement of winter when so many scents vanish, when the cold numbs our nostrils and only the strongest smell gets through. Clay insists on brick and stone to house it, and squeezes plants dry to find scents to freshen the inevitable staleness of closed doors and windows. The sweet smell of your beloved's hot skin as they sleep, with you just woken at their side.

'Touch. Wet leaves, rough bark, smooth silk, warm fur, another person's flesh, cotton sheets. Clear a wood and build a house and fill it with things whose texture recalls earth and grass and leaves and branches. Take metal from the heart of the earth and fashion it smooth, carve it to run your fingertips over, to please your eye. The curve of a jug to recall a smooth stone, the bole of a tree.

'Taste. Plunder the world for herbs and spices and fruits and vegetables and meats to please the palate! More than the necessary fuel for the body, make of it an art form. Cordon bleu — the decadent delight of global choice is a phone call away. Enjoy the taste of your lover's lips, her lovely sweat.

'Hearing. Voices, wind in the trees, music at the press of a button. That voice which says I love you and means it, the laughter of love, the teasing, sharing sounds that go beyond words. It's all a living circle — a spiral.

'Five senses interweaving through every cell of life pulsing on this planet, giving the clay beings experiences of endless pleasure. Other people! What a dazzling web to hold our spirits, reckless about the spider of decay waiting out of sight as she ravels us in.

'We are born torn apart: the clay in fear of its own mortality, the spirit yearning to regain its immortality. The body is in harness to the spirit, the spirit is in chains of skin and bone and time. Life is learning to live in harmony with our divided selves. Knowing yourself so that there is no space between thoughts and actions. Everything has its price and the — foolish — first immortals traded their ethereal foreverness for five senses and a green planet to play on. Nowadays, it seems like a bad bargain, in the global scene, with famines and cruelty and greed and pollution and genocide.'

She looked at me again, and her face was bright with colour.

'But when I take a walk,' she said very quietly, 'a walk in a wood,' she smiled, 'when I walk with my lover, hold her hand, hear the stream, see the birds, taste the wild grasses, smell the flowers in the sun, it is all worthwhile.

'Because this time round, I have the nostalgia of one who will be leaving somewhere very dear to my heart. So dear that I know it by heart. I will hold every memory of this living in my spirit, I have learnt so much, I have so much to learn, but I am aware that I will not pass this way again and, this time, a door has opened somewhere so that I have been allowed to see that all the time there are choices and it is up to me to choose right.

'Yes,' she said, 'I will be leaving somewhere I love with both body and spirit, and going somewhere I yearn to be. Will you stay with me for a while? Thank you. Bring those roses close to my face and pour me some wine. You are so kind. Sit beside me and hold my hand while I look into your eyes.'

We sat until all I could see were two bright points of light swimming in twin pools of darkness. She pressed my hand.

She said: 'There's one last thing I'd like. Would you — would you sing me an old-fashioned love song?'

Her words were light and alive with yearning.

I sang until my heart and the dawn were breaking.